IN THE SHADOW
OF DARKNESS

By the Author

Secrets in a Small Town

In the Shadow of Darkness

Visit us at www.boldstrokesbooks.com

IN THE SHADOW
OF DARKNESS

by

Nicole Stiling

2020

IN THE SHADOW OF DARKNESS

ISBN 13: 978-1-63555-624-7

THIS TRADE PAPERBACK ORIGINAL IS PUBLISHED BY
BOLD STROKES BOOKS, INC.
P.O. BOX 249
VALLEY FALLS, NY 12185

FIRST EDITION: FEBRUARY 2020

CREDITS
EDITORS: VICTORIA VILLASEÑOR AND CINDY CRESAP
PRODUCTION DESIGN: STACIA SEAMAN
COVER DESIGN BY TAMMY SEIDICK

Acknowledgments

A heartfelt thank you to the entire Bold Strokes Books family. You run the terrifying process of publishing like a well-oiled machine. Thank you for everything.

To my editor, Victoria—you make everything better.

To the family and friends who have supported me and read all of my works—no matter how far outside their usual genre—I couldn't have done this without you.

To my wife—for her love, patience, and encouragement. You are the hero of my story.

CHAPTER ONE

Lowell, Massachusetts, 1926

Angeline Miles had walked this route every night for the last year and had never been spooked, even on nights when there were no stars in the sky to light her path. But something felt off. She felt like she was being watched. Like someone was following her along Pawtucket Boulevard, weaving in and out of the trees like an illusionist. She stopped, listening for footsteps or rustling as she scanned the road behind her. Nothing.

The rest of the walk home took less time than usual. Her steps were quicker and tighter than normal under the dark November sky. Darkness was falling earlier and earlier these days, and soon Benjamin would insist on picking her up at the machine shop. It had taken so long to convince him that some light secretarial work would be advantageous to her state of mind that Angeline wasn't going to fight him if he insisted on driving her home once winter had taken its stranglehold on the sun. Though she did enjoy her walks very much. It was her private time to think, to just be.

She tightened her wool coat around her as she quickened her step, the feeling of being watched growing stronger. She felt a tiny tear in the satin lining of the pocket. She'd have to sew that right away. That coat had cost twenty-five dollars and ninety-five cents at Sears, so it had to last for, at the very least, the remainder of her twenties.

Out on the river, there was a man in a canoe drifting near the shore, bundled up like it was the dead of winter instead of late autumn. Angeline strained to see what the man was doing, but it looked like he was fast asleep with a fishing line bobbing lazily along the surface. Maybe that was it. Maybe she was just hearing the sounds of the river.

Like most evenings this time of year, the street was deserted. Angeline walked past Mrs. Dudley's rooming house and saw the elderly woman leaning over her front porch railing, closing and fastening the shutters.

"Evening, Mrs. Dudley," Angeline called, and felt a little better at the sound of her own voice in the stillness around her.

"Hello there, Mrs. Miles. Going to be a cold one tonight," Mrs. Dudley said, rubbing her shoulders for effect.

"Sure is. Feels pretty chilly now if you ask me." Angeline shivered and waved again on her way past the house. A small part of her wanted to stop, to make conversation, to ask Mrs. Dudley if she could come in for a cup of tea. But that was silly. It was suppertime, it was cold, and Angeline wasn't about to let a little case of the creeps turn her into a frightened child.

Her house was just around the bend, fifty yards at most. Angeline clutched her pocketbook to her chest and finally felt her anxiety begin to subside when she saw the soft glow of her porch light, beckoning to her in the navy blue darkness.

A cold wind swept by, sending a fresh shiver through her. She broke out into a jog, her pumps chafing her ankles. So close…

It happened so fast Angeline had no idea what had hit her. She felt herself lifted from the ground, an unknown entity gripping her from behind. Before she reached her front steps, her breath was taken from her by a hard blow to her midsection.

"Benj—" she screamed, before she felt a cold hand clamp over her mouth.

"Scream again and I will kill you."

Strangely, the voice sounded distinctly feminine. She tried kicking her legs against the attacker, but before she understood what was happening, she was on the ground, looking into the thick brush of a maple tree, the woods around her quiet and ominous. She was no longer in front of her house, but in the thicket across the way. They were surrounded by nature on all sides.

"Who are you?" she asked, panic threatening to take over. "What do you want?"

"My name is Kathryn. I was going to drink your blood. I haven't decided." She put her hand on her hip, her face expressionless.

Angeline's eyes widened. The woman was still cloaked in darkness, but she could make out some of her features. Her hair was long and crimson. It flowed down her back like red silk. She wore what looked like a man's suit, though her frame was slight. She was a sickly shade of pale that made it look like she was glowing against the darkness around her.

"I don't know what you're trying to pull here, but my husband, Benjamin, is close by and he'll have you locked up for this! Let me go now and I won't tell him!" Angeline tried to sound confident and in control, but her voice shook with fear.

Kathryn laughed. "Ooh, Benjamin," she mocked. She pretended to chew on her nails anxiously before she tossed her head back and laughed. "Trust me, Angeline, Benjamin is no match for me. If you manage to drag him into this, know that his death will be on you."

Angeline tried to scurry backward into a sitting position. Her skirt scrunched up against the back of her thighs. "How do you know my name? If money is what you're after, I can assure you I don't have much with me. A few coins, I think. You're welcome to them," she said, searching her bag for her wallet.

Kathryn stilled Angeline's hand with her own. "I don't want your money. I want you. I think." She stood, looking down at

Angeline with a furrowed brow. "I've gone back and forth. I don't like to mix business with pleasure, but I might make an exception in this case."

"Business? What are you talking about?"

Kathryn sighed. "The business of existing. I usually do my business and move on. But you were ripe for the picking, walking home alone every night. I've had my eye on you for some time. Doesn't seem like a very smart decision, a sweet girl like you, on the streets by yourself. In the dark."

Angeline stiffened. Even in peril, her independence vowed to make itself known. "I'll have you know that I've been walking places on my own since I was nine years old. I don't need anyone to chaperone me, Mrs...?"

"Kathryn," she repeated. "Are you sure about that? A chaperone might have been a good idea," Kathryn said, gesturing between herself and Angeline.

"Are you going to kill me?" Angeline's voice sounded small and weak, but she didn't care. She just wanted to go home, fall into bed, and cry.

"I don't think so. I've been lonely and I could use a friend," Kathryn said, shrugging as though it was the most normal thing in the world.

"Okay," Angeline said, clearing her throat. She had no idea what this insane woman was going on about, but maybe if she changed her tactic she could get out of this unscathed. "Then I will be your friend. We can meet up some night to play gin rummy? Or cribbage, if you prefer?"

Kathryn laughed again. "Not that kind of friend. Someone to travel the world with. Someone to confide in. Someone who will understand me. Someone who can relate to me."

Angeline cocked her head. "I'm not sure I understand what you mean."

And then Kathryn was on her, a blur of terrifying motion. Angeline heard the soft squish of teeth against flesh before she felt the searing pain in her neck. She tried to swat at the back of

Kathryn's head, to pull her hair, to buck her off. Nothing worked. Before long, the pain melted into a kind of intense pressure, gradually turning into a steady, hard pulse at the side of her neck. She tried to stay conscious. She tried to keep her head above water, but the pull was too strong. It was easier to close her eyes, to let go…

❖

The sound of scurrying brought her from the depths of the abyss. Leaves crunching. Angeline opened her eyes and turned her head in time to see a raccoon disappear into the thicket. The motion of turning her head nearly caused her to cry out. She was so stiff. How long had she been out there? Angeline tried to lift her head, and it felt like she had slammed it against a metal pole. She rested it against the cool grass and tried to focus. The sky was dark. Where was she? Who was she? No answers came.

Her head began to spin. She couldn't tell if she was spinning or if it was the world around her, somehow off its axis and spiraling toward a gruesome finish. She squeezed her eyes shut to stave off the nausea, to try to steady herself. It worked for the most part, but the spinning still came in spurts. *Maybe this is death. This is what it feels like to die.* The thought wasn't as terrifying as she assumed it would be. The darkness, the loneliness that she felt, threatened to swallow her whole. She tried to take comfort in the onyx blanket that surrounded her.

But no. She couldn't be dying. When she opened her eyes again, everything was vibrant, detailed. Everything around her was too alive for this to be death. The sounds, the sights, even the taste of dirt and leaves and sap emblazoned within her. She forced herself into a sitting position against a tree. She blinked repeatedly, hoping something, anything, would come back to her.

Slowly, her life began to creep in, tiny bits at a time. Her name was Angeline Vallencourt. Miles, actually. *That's right.* Benjamin Miles was her husband. They lived in a small but modern house on Varnum Avenue. Her sister, Stella, was jealous of their automatic Maytag washing machine. Benjamin liked to use a piece of white bread to sop up any leftover gravy from his plate. She didn't like gravy. She was Mr. Grady's secretary at the machine shop. She was twenty-six years old.

As she stood, holding on to the base of the tree, the attack came back to her, sudden and jarring. A crazy woman named Kathryn had abducted her and cut her throat. Or something like that. Angeline reached up to her neck to see if she was bleeding. She wasn't. She felt two small puncture wounds beneath her ear. They didn't hurt, exactly, but they tingled when she touched them.

She made her way out of the woods in a trancelike state and hobbled down the street, slow and unsteady. She didn't hurt, exactly, but her bones felt like they were struggling not to disintegrate. She was lucky to be alive, and she kept repeating that phrase in her head as though she were trying to convince herself. Her coat was covered in twigs and leaves and the heel of her left shoe had snapped off. She dug her key out of her pocketbook and entered the foyer. She was home. It looked like home. It smelled like home.

But it didn't feel like home.

The haunting melody of Irving Kaufman's "Tonight You Belong to Me" floated out from the parlor. She could hear Benjamin turning the rotary dial on their telephone.

"Benjamin?" Her voice didn't sound like her own. Weaker. Lost.

"Oh, thank you anyway, she's just arrived home."

Benjamin ran into the foyer, his tie hanging around his neck like an honors stole. "Angeline! Where have you been? I was worried sick!"

"You don't need to shout, Benjamin," Angeline said, fighting the urge to cover her ears. "I was attacked and left for dead in the woods over by Clay Pit Brook. I'm lucky the animals didn't get to me."

He rushed over to her and wrapped Angeline in a tight hug, though her arms hung at her side. She wanted to hug him back, but her arms just swayed limply. She felt numb. "Shall I get you a cup of tea? Or something stronger, like coffee? I'll call the police right away."

Angeline turned toward the stairs without a word, slowly making her way up to her bedroom. She stared straight ahead, everything that had once been a source of security now cold and unfamiliar. She wanted to turn to Benjamin for comfort but found she couldn't. He no longer felt like comfort, though she couldn't interpret exactly why. The face of that woman kept appearing in her peripheral vision, like a demented hologram. She clutched her pocketbook to her chest and ran her fingers over the wound beneath her ear. "Not necessary, Benjamin. My attacker is long gone, I'm certain of it. There's nothing they could do at this point, and I don't want to spend the rest of the night in a police station. I'm tired and sore and I think I'd like to be alone for a bit. I'm sure I just need a good night's sleep and I'll be right as rain." They wouldn't believe a woman had taken her, dragged her away, and left her. Women didn't do that kind of thing, and Angeline would end up locked away. Better to put the whole thing behind her.

CHAPTER TWO

Fog Hollow, Massachusetts, current day

"Dammit," Megan Denham said, inspecting the fingernail on her index finger. A chunk of nail had broken off and was hanging on by a thread. She peeled it off and sighed. So much for the forty-dollar gel manicure the salon had advertised as "virtually unbreakable." She clicked the trigger on the gas nozzle a few more times, trying to eke out every bit of the twenty dollars she had added to her tank. She replaced the nozzle and slid into the front seat of her Escape.

She searched her purse for her keys but came up empty-handed. She looked on the floor, the seat, and on the ground near the open door. Nothing.

"Really?" Megan threw her head back against the headrest. She had a vague memory of placing her keys on the counter when she gave the clerk a twenty-dollar bill. She closed her car door a little harder than she meant to and walked toward the small convenience store. There was a black pickup truck parked out front.

As soon as she walked in, she saw her dolphin-shaped key chain that spelled out *Cape Cod* sitting in front of the gum display. "Just forgot my keys," she said to no one in particular. The clerk stared at her wide-eyed. He had both hands up in a gesture of surrender. He looked terrified, but there was no one else at the counter. Megan raised her eyebrows.

"Is everything okay?"

"Get on the ground. Now."

Megan whipped around to see a twentysomething man with shaggy blond hair and unruly facial hair walking up the aisle past the chips and popcorn. He had a pistol in his hand, pointed their way. His hand was trembling slightly.

"Okay. Please don't shoot." *This isn't happening.* Megan sank slowly to her knees, not wanting to set the shooter off with any sudden movements. She was suddenly thrust into an episode of any crime show, ever, and that sense of unreality threatened to overtake her. She blinked rapidly.

"All the way down." His voice was gruff and deep.

"Okay."

Megan sank onto her stomach, her arms splayed above her head like she was flying. She noticed an ant at eye level, heading toward the store exit carrying a pretzel crumb on his back. She envied his freedom.

"Empty the cash register into a plastic bag. And put a few rolls of scratch tickets in there too."

The clerk, a balding man in an oxford shirt with two pens sticking out of his breast pocket, nodded nervously. "Do you want everything in the safe too?"

"Yeah, empty the safe."

Megan breathed shallowly, cautiously optimistic that she might make it out of this alive after all. She thought of her aunt making beef barley soup, packing more than Megan could ever possibly eat into a giant Tupperware container. She thought of her cat, Merlin, sprawled out on the back of the couch waiting for her. She knew her cell phone was in her pocket, but she didn't dare move. Just let the degenerate take the money and get the hell out.

The cash register dinged as the clerk opened it. Megan could hear the shuffling of dollar bills and the scratching of paper as the clerk stuffed a paper bag with the items that the thief had asked for.

"I'll open the safe now."

Out of the corner of her eye, Megan saw the clerk bend over. He stood up quickly with a double-barrel shotgun pointed at the gunman, but by the time he'd cocked it, the thief had regained his focus and pulled the trigger. Megan screamed as the clerk let out a moan and collapsed to the ground.

"You stupid fuck!" the thief shouted, rushing the counter. A package of Twinkies fell out of his pocket. He snatched the bag off the counter and pointed his gun at Megan. She'd scrambled to her knees when the gun had gone off.

"Just go! You have the money, I won't say anything!" Megan yelled, covering the back of her head with her hands. Panic flooded through her in great waves and tears blurred her vision. "Please!"

"You know what I look like, you dumb bitch! I have no choice!"

Megan heard the deafening sound of the gunshot, and in the split second before she crumpled to the ground, she wondered if dying was going to hurt as much as she thought it would.

❖

The sound of her blood pumping brought Megan out of the darkness. She tasted something metallic on her lips, and she could feel the weight of another person on top of her.

"Just a little more," the disembodied voice commanded. "Come on."

Megan felt her chest constrict, then she gulped a mouthful of air. Repeatedly, until she felt like she could breathe normally again. Her eyes opened and she tried to regain control.

"Where am I? What happened?" she asked, panting.

"You were hurt."

"Yes, I figured that out, but what are you doing?" Megan asked, looking at the stranger's bleeding wrist.

"Saving you?" she said, sounding the slightest bit annoyed.

"Why are you bleeding? Are *you* hurt?" Megan felt her pulse quicken as she realized she wasn't in the gas station anymore. Instead, she was lying on the fringes of a department store parking lot, bleeding from an apparent wound in her stomach, while this woman appeared to also be bleeding out.

She looked at her wrist, then turned it over quickly. "Yes, I'm hurt. Sure. So, best of luck. Godspeed. Get well soon." The woman stood, brushing the dirt off of her jeans.

"No, wait. You can't just leave me here! Was I...shot?" Megan asked, recalling the events of the gas station. She looked down at the blood on her top and pulled up her shirt.

"Yes."

"Oh my God, I was shot. Why didn't you take me to a hospital?" Megan searched for her wound but found that underneath the smear of blood there was no bullet hole. She opened her sweater and lifted her shirt to poke and prod at her stomach.

"You would have died."

"What do you mean? There's nothing here. The bullet must have just grazed me." Megan tried to stand, but she was woozy. The woman reached out to steady her, placing a hand on Megan's forearm.

"Okay, then. My bad."

"Who are you?"

The woman sighed heavily and rubbed the back of her neck. "Angeline. If you're all set, I'm gonna go."

"Did you kidnap me or something? What are we doing out here?"

"My *God*! Look, you would have died from a gunshot wound if I'd left you in that store or if I had called an ambulance. You didn't even have a pulse when I got there. I was too late for the cashier. And the guy that shot you, well, he's dead too. I saw you, and I didn't want you to die, so I fed you a little of my blood to heal you. I'm not going to turn you or anything. That's it. Can I go now?" Angeline raised her eyebrows and crossed her arms. "You fed me your *blood*? Okay, so you're psychotic? Or just a goth who's taken things a little too far?" Megan took a few steps backward, realizing that poking someone who was clearly mentally unstable might not be in her best interest.

Angeline laughed and looked up at the sky. "Yeah, that's it. I'm a psychotic goth. Next time I'll just mind my own business. Make sure you have a doctor remove the bullet. I don't know what kind of long-term effect that could have on you."

Megan opened her mouth to remind her that there was no gunshot, but before she could say another word, Angeline had taken off. She'd jogged toward the tree line and then seemingly disappeared. Megan looked around the empty parking lot to see if there was a car parked along the woods or maybe across the street. The only vehicle she saw was an eighteen-wheeler parked at the far end of the lot, the driver sleeping comfortably at the wheel.

How the hell did she get us out here? Megan patted her pocket, and thankfully, her cell phone was still there. She was still unsettled and sore, but at least she hadn't lost her connection to safety. She wondered if she'd sustained a head injury and this was some bizarre hallucination. Maybe she'd walked to the store in a daze? Maybe she just needed to rest. She pulled out the phone and started to dial 9-1-1. But before she hit send, she disconnected instead. What would she tell them? Why was she out here, in the Bullseye parking lot of all places? She dialed her friend Stacey instead. She seemed like the safer option.

Stacey answered the phone groggily after a few rings.

Megan's voice sounded high-pitched, but she couldn't help it. "You are not going to believe what happened to me tonight. Can you come get me and bring me to my car? I know what time it is. Just trust me. Pick me up in the Bullseye parking lot."

The Bullseye was about a mile or so away from the gas station where the shooting had taken place. It didn't make any sense. How had Angeline gotten them there without a car? Why didn't she just stay and wait for the police? Maybe she was wanted. Some outlaw who happened to be in the wrong place at the wrong time. And how had she healed her? Did she really heal her or was she just crazy? Megan felt her stomach again. There was a slight discomfort, but no real pain. She remembered the gunman pointing his gun at her and pulling the trigger. She remembered the second of debilitating pain before she had blacked out. But it *must* have only grazed her, right? Obviously, if she'd been shot, she'd be in agony. The woman must have been mistaken. Crazy.

Still in her haze of hollow delusion, Megan couldn't deny that there was something intriguing about Angeline. She was beautiful, with long wavy brown hair and dreamlike eyes the color of honey, but it was more than that. There was something almost preternatural about her, something…feral. And did Angeline say that the clerk was dead, and so was the shooter? Megan shook her head forcefully, trying to clear away some of the cobwebs. When she finally saw Stacey's Civic pull into the parking lot, she fought the urge to cry in relief.

CHAPTER THREE

Great Barrington, Massachusetts, 1926

Angeline woke up on a box spring with a coil poking her side. She sat up quickly and clutched the scratchy wool blanket to her chest.

"You're awake. I tried not to disturb you," Kathryn said, a small lantern beside her. She shook out the match she was holding until the flame disappeared.

"Where are we?" Angeline asked, trying to identify the vast space around them.

Kathryn shrugged. "A warehouse. Grains, I think. There's a lot of these things lying around the floor and some hay up at the entrance. Seems like it's been empty for quite some time." She held up a sandy-colored pellet.

"Why are we here?"

"I just thought we should be somewhere secluded for a while. Sometimes those that are…" she paused, "recently turned, you know, choke. Panic. Cause a scene. I just wanted to make sure that you were calm and collected."

Angeline cleared her throat. Kathryn insinuating that she might panic was causing her to panic. "I don't remember much. Once you came and took me from my house the night after, well, you know, everything got sort of foggy. What's happening again?"

Kathryn exuded nothing but patience. "That can happen in the beginning. A lot of things won't make sense, and then suddenly, they'll make complete sense. Trust me on that. I came for you that night because you and I are friends now. Eternal friends," she said with a light laugh. "I turned you into a vampire. Like me. Remember?"

She did remember. The memory and the horror of it nearly overwhelmed Angeline's senses. She suddenly understood why Kathryn had taken her to this place. The urge to scream was staggering.

"Oh, it's not so bad," Kathryn said. "There are a lot of perks to immortality."

Angeline said nothing, but she was sure that the look of terror she imagined in her eyes needed no explanation. The walk home, the bite, the capture, the first drink of blood that Kathryn had brought to her once she'd calmed down. She remembered the rapture that the first sips had provided and felt an alarming sense of ease.

"For example, you're a lot stronger now. And the older you get, the stronger you'll become. Your vision is crisper, clearer. Your hearing has improved. And you won't die," Kathryn said. She spoke the last sentence with a bright smile and a gleam in her eye.

"We're indestructible?" Angeline asked. Her voice sounded a little loud in her ears. She couldn't tell if it was the enhanced hearing Kathryn was talking about or a psychosomatic symptom.

Kathryn sat on the edge of the box spring and pulled her legs into a loose cross-legged position. "Not entirely. Most of the lore that you've heard isn't true. But some of it is. If we're turned to ash, either by fire or too much sunlight, or if we're separated from our heads, that's it. It's over. But as long as you're careful, those things are fairly easy to avoid."

"Am I dead?" Angeline asked. The fear she'd pushed away earlier returned in full force.

Kathryn cocked her head. "Technically, yes."

Angeline gasped, fighting for air that seemed to flee from her.

"But not *really* dead," Kathryn said quickly. "Look at yourself. You're moving and talking and able to think like any other living being. You're just...different. Somewhere between living and dead."

"I need to call my husband. He must be worried sick. And my parents! They've probably gone mad with nerves. Do you know where there's a telephone close by?" Angeline tried to stand, but her legs turned to jelly. She sank down onto the box spring.

"Whoa, whoa, whoa, kid. You can't just jump up and expect to run a marathon. Your body is in transition. It's a delicate process. And besides, you can't talk to your husband. Or your family. Ever again. Remember?" Kathryn looked toward one of the cracked windows.

Angeline rubbed her face with her hands. Maybe this was all a nightmare. She just needed to wake up.

"It'll become easier, I promise. You have a lot to learn, and luckily, a lot of time to learn it in. For now, lie down. You need your rest."

Before Angeline could protest or ask more questions, Kathryn extinguished the lantern and they were once again bathed in blackness.

❖

Angeline sat in the passenger seat of Kathryn's Star Six Coupe, toying with the stitching on the seat. She leaned her head against the window while she waited for Kathryn to return.

She'd only been away from home for a few short months, but to Angeline, it felt like a lifetime. She tried to push the recurring sad thoughts away, thoughts of her parents, her friends, Benjamin. She'd only been afforded a brief good-bye with her loved ones before Kathryn had come back for her, and they couldn't even know that it was good-bye. She closed her eyes, pushing away the guilt that consumed her when she thought of them searching for her. They must have been sick with worry. She fidgeted in her seat, willing the heaviness to retreat, even just for a while. It was easier to focus on the freedom and the abandon that this new life afforded her. And *that* was easiest when she was with Kathryn, her only beacon of consistency. Angeline felt some of her tension fade when she saw Kathryn approach the car.

"Hi," Kathryn said, as she slipped into the driver's seat. "For you." She handed Angeline a nickel-plated thermos.

Angeline felt her body twitch with excitement as she unscrewed the lid. She gulped down the entire contents of the thermos in less than a minute.

"Easy, tiger. Although I can understand why. It's not every day I'm able to take down a virile—"

"Stop!" Angeline interrupted. "You know I don't want to know about it. It's easier for me to pretend you purchased it at the market."

Kathryn turned to Angeline, her eyes flashing. "But I didn't. And you know I didn't. You need to embrace your true self, Angeline. The quicker, the better."

"I don't know what you're implying, but this is my true self, Kathryn. I didn't ask you to make me like this. I'm not as callous as you, and I doubt I ever will be."

Kathryn laughed bitterly. "We can talk about it again in a hundred or so years, and I'll watch you eat your judgmental words." She paused. "In fact, why wait? From this point on, you're on your own. No more room service. You can hunt right along with me, or you don't eat. Sound like a plan?"

Angeline sat straight up. "You know I can't do that."

"Why not?"

"Kathryn, don't do this. You don't always have to be so righteous! I wasn't questioning your methods, I was just saying that you have a callousness about you that I don't have. Yet. I'm sure I will someday, but I can't do what you do." Angeline tucked a piece of hair behind her ear nervously. She'd seen a few glimpses of Kathryn's ire over their short time together, but never directed squarely at her. It was usually at the humans.

"You can, and you will. You're a killer, Angeline. It's what we do. If you want to start on something small, like a rabbit, that's fine. But you'll have to move up eventually."

"No!" Angeline yelled. "I can't kill a rabbit! Do I have to kill someone to eat? Can't I just, you know, take what I need and let them be?"

Kathryn looked thoughtful. "Yes. That's what I do most of the time. But the hunger will kick in, and it's a practiced resistance to stop when you've had your fill. It's not as easy as it sounds."

Angeline felt anxiety well up within her. "I'll learn. But for now, let's just keep it the way it is. I'll earn my keep another way. I can steal or forage or do whatever you need me to do."

Kathryn touched her knee gently. "No."

Rage bubbled through her, a welcome substitute to the aching sadness of most of her days. "Then I'm done with you. You can't treat me like I'm your underling or some idiot pupil." Angeline opened the car door angrily and stormed off into the woods, unaware of where she would go, but not really caring.

Angeline gasped as Kathryn appeared directly in front of her. "You're not done with me until I'm done with *you*. You really think you can make it out here on your own? In the wilderness of western Massachusetts, where everyone eyes you just a little differently and you make people just slightly uncomfortable? But no one can really pinpoint why, can they? They just know something is *off*. That *you* are off. And with your laughably squeamish stomach, you'll starve before the month is out. I've seen a starving vampire, and trust me, you don't want to live like that. The flesh actually dries up and flicks off like paper. What little blood is left starts to trickle out the pores. The lips peel back into a permanent, horrifying smile. And yet, they live. You think you can do it without me? Be my guest." Kathryn flashed her teeth at Angeline, her lip curled into a snarl.

Angeline wasn't sure if she had ever hated anyone as she

hated Kathryn in that moment. She felt her soul wilt as she realized that Kathryn had a point. Angeline didn't know how to survive in the wilderness, or even outside a city, really. She'd never even gotten the chance to go camping.

"You're right, Kathryn," Angeline said. She sighed sadly as she walked back to the shiny red coupe.

❖

Thirteen days. Thirteen days, nine hours, and seventeen minutes since Angeline had eaten. She curled up on the stiff bed inside the hotel room, her stomach cramping with pain. She was ravenous, but she decided that she'd rather die than drink from a living vein. Maybe death would be the best outcome she could hope for. Maybe if she proved to Kathryn that she wouldn't eat, if she became a burden, Kathryn would leave her in the sunlight to die properly. She didn't want to be the monster that Kathryn was showing herself to be. Besides, there wasn't much for Angeline to live for anymore. Everything she'd loved had been taken away, and all the travel and power in the world couldn't make up for the emptiness that she battled. But what if the abyss that awaited her was much worse? She didn't necessarily believe in a fiery pit of an afterlife (though her former pastor would clutch his head in horror if he knew that), but that didn't shake the concern of *what if*. And if it was just a never-ending void of blackness, was she ready to cast herself into it? Angeline chastised herself for being a coward. She just needed a damn drink. But Kathryn never wavered. Not once did she see the anguish in Angeline's eyes and satiate her hunger with a simple thermos. She could have so easily erased the pain, but she chose not to.

"What's cookin', good lookin'?" Kathryn asked as she sauntered into the room. Her colorful gingham dress swayed slightly as she tossed her cloche into a chair by the door. She fastened the chain and set a brown paper bag on the small table.

Angeline ignored her.

"I brought some food."

Angeline didn't even look up. The first time Kathryn had said that, Angeline nearly mauled her looking for it. But it turned out to be a container of shepherd's pie that Kathryn had picked up at a local restaurant. Angeline ate it all, hoping against hope that it would relieve some of her hunger. Her taste buds hadn't changed. The mashed potatoes and corn and peas glided down her throat like silk. But it did nothing for the hunger. If anything, it made it worse.

"I don't want it," Angeline said. Her voice was weak.

"Aw come, on, I bought us some cream cheese sandwiches, on that brown bread that you like." Kathryn rustled the bag and put the two small packages on the table.

"Kathryn, I'm dying. I don't want any fucking cream cheese sandwiches."

Kathryn froze and didn't say a word. Angeline raised her eyebrow, challenging her even from her fetal position on the bed. Angeline never used foul language. On the odd times when Kathryn would slip, Angeline made it a point to cringe and *tsk-tsk* her.

Seeming to regain her composure, Kathryn sat on the edge of Angeline's bed. "You don't have to live like this. You can cure what ails you in five minutes flat. Just say the word and I'll show you what to do."

"No."

"Your stubbornness can only take you so far, Angeline. You really will wither away if you don't eat something soon."

"I don't care." If she'd felt better, Angeline would have been bothered by her own petulance.

"Then I've done all I can." Kathryn touched Angeline's ankle, but Angeline swiftly pulled it away. "Let me know if you change your mind."

"If this leads to my death in some way, I hope you carry that guilt around for the rest of eternity. You're a monster. A real, live monster."

"Eh, I'll get over it," Kathryn said, throwing Angeline a wink. She sat down and unwrapped her sandwich. "Delicious."

❖

On her fifteenth day without any type of sustenance, Angeline began to lose blood. It teared from her eyes in crimson streaks down her face. Her teeth became loose. She had no feeling in her extremities. Her stomach was so hollow she felt like it had folded in on itself.

The Barrington Bedside Motel was probably the third motel they'd been in that month. There was no reason to leave until an employee or neighboring guest started to take too much of an interest. Angeline imagined it was hard not to, especially since she embodied the pale face of death. Not to mention that she was traveling with an ethereal beauty in her own right, and two women traipsing around the countryside without a chaperone wasn't exactly the norm.

They had talked about getting an apartment, going somewhere warmer. But that had all been before. Since Angeline had refused to hunt for her own food, the only conversations between them were terse and matter-of-fact.

Angeline knew she couldn't go on like this. Either Kathryn needed to kill her, or she needed to find food. Kathryn was out, performing her nightly ritual of God-knows-what, and showed no inclination to end Angeline's misery. The agony was proving to be too much, and she chastised herself for being weak. If she could just take the edge off, then maybe she could think clearly again. Decide what she wanted to do. She could have simply walked out into the sunlight, but she found she was unable take such an ultimate step on her own. In the meantime, she had to do something to make the pain subside, even just a little. Angeline dragged herself out of bed, her clothes musty and wrinkled. She looked at herself in the mirror; she was little more than an apparition. She startled at her reflection. She was frightened of herself.

The motel was deserted. Their room was on the second floor, a white metal railing the only thing protecting Angeline from plummeting to the pavement below. She cast a glance toward it, twice, wondering if a fall would kill her. Maybe it would at least maim her in such a way that she would be unable to walk or stand, and someone would find her and do the job for her. It would save her from scavenging for food like an emaciated coyote. But something within her persisted, and she continued making her way toward the flickering light of the motel sign. She was unsteady on her feet and clung to the flimsy banister as she crept down the stairs.

She tried to lick her lips, but her mouth was dry. She limped her way through the clearing in the brush behind the motel. The wind was strong that night, and the creak of the motel sign swinging back and forth on its hinges caused Angeline to shudder. She couldn't help but snicker at the irony. She was now the thing that people feared lurking in the dark. There was nothing, no man or beast that could pose a threat to her now. In her current state, that certainly wasn't the case, but she'd seen Kathryn take down a two-hundred-pound boxer like a lion felling a gazelle. It was the last time she witnessed Kathryn kill. She just couldn't bear it.

She made her way through the sharp twigs and pine needles, searching for something that would make her well. She wouldn't have admitted it, even to herself, but she was looking for a corpse. She was looking for an animal who'd met their unfortunate demise through the actions of another animal or a hunter with shaky aim. She sniffed deeply for the pungent scent of blood and followed a trail farther into the woods.

There, she found a bird, maybe a raven, maybe a crow, she couldn't really tell the difference. The bird had no wounds on him, so it was entirely possible he'd just died of old age and Angeline wouldn't have to interrupt the natural balance at all.

She protracted her fangs, a voluntary action she was still coming to terms with, and began to drink.

For a moment, the rush of blood down the back of her throat provided her the bliss she'd been deprived of. She savored it, shooting up a silent prayer to anyone who would listen that the feeling would continue indefinitely.

And then it stopped. Before she knew what was happening, Angeline felt the bird stripped from her hands and she fell backward onto the ground. Kathryn stood above her, irate.

"What the hell are you doing? Was this thing dead when you found it? Answer me!" Kathryn's eyes blazed fire.

Angeline would have if she could have. Her throat began to burn, and her stomach churned. With one hand, she grabbed her throat, and with the other, she pressed on her stomach.

"You can't feed from something dead, Angeline. Any more than a few minutes after the heart stops pumping, and the blood becomes poison. Your blood will turn toxic!"

Angeline thought that was a very real probability. The pain she'd felt in her stomach from hunger was nothing compared to the pain that shot throughout her body. She retched, but even the expulsion of the poisoned blood didn't relieve the pain.

"You need strength to fight this off, Angeline. I'll let you die. Right here, right now. I'll do it for you. I can take your pain away. Do you want to die, Angeline?" Kathryn knelt beside her, cradling her head between her hands. "Do you want to die? Or do you want to live?"

Her eyes began to close of their own accord. She could see the trees that surrounded them fading from view, as though her mind had accepted that this was the end. But it didn't feel like it should have felt. It wasn't like being swaddled; it was more like being snuffed out. Eradicated. She wasn't ready. Goddamn it, she couldn't let go. Angeline opened her mouth, but a sick croak came out instead of anything coherent. She tried again. "Live."

The next thing she knew, Angeline was in Kathryn's arms, speeding through the trees at breakneck pace. At least it felt that way. When they finally stopped, Angeline's head swam. Her vision came into focus. They were watching a campfire, where a young man and a young woman were roasting frankfurters on long sticks over the open flame. Angeline decided they couldn't have been more than twenty.

"Live, Angeline. Live." Kathryn's voice hissed into Angeline's ear, more of a command than encouragement.

Angeline began to cry, and the tears spilled over her cheeks. She felt her teeth scrape against her bottom lip. For the first time in weeks, her body was responding to stimulus, and she could nearly hear the blood coursing through the couple's veins. She didn't want to do it. She didn't want to cross that invisible line. How could she without loathing herself?

She closed her eyes and leapt. Something feral took over, and when she opened her eyes, she had the young woman on the ground, her eyes panicked and her feet kicking, but even in a weakened state Angeline was able to hold her down. She buried her teeth into the soft flesh of the woman's neck, right above her collarbone. As the blood filled her, Angeline felt herself leave her body, euphoria elevating her to a different plane. She could feel herself healing from the inside out. She had the sudden urge to laugh, to scream. But she couldn't tear herself away from the woman. She drank until there was nothing left.

"You are supposed to always be aware of your surroundings. I took care of the male, but if I hadn't, I'm pretty sure he would have shoved a torch up your ass. Next time make sure you don't leave yourself vulnerable." Kathryn wiped her lips, a tiny dab of red still resting on her chin.

Angeline looked back to the woman. She lay there unmoving, her body twisted unnaturally. "I killed her, didn't I?" she asked, still on her knees.

"I would say so." Kathryn jabbed at the body with the toe of her boot. "Yes, she's dead."

Angeline picked up the small satchel the woman had left on the makeshift bench they'd been sitting on. Her identification card was crumpled and well-worn. "Margaret Bursley. Authorized to enter the archives building during the normal operating hours." Angeline read the card aloud and nodded to herself. This wasn't just a body, an empty vessel of blood to satiate Angeline's hunger. This was a person. With a name and a job and maybe even a family. A life. "I'm a killer now."

"You've been a killer for a while. You've just decided to act on your instincts. It's your nature. Nothing more. You wouldn't call a lion a killer, would you? A bear?" Kathryn lifted the body of the young man and placed it onto the fire. "If you can dispose of the evidence, it's always best to do so. We don't need the nuisance of police officers searching for a murderer."

Angeline watched in horror as Kathryn worked quickly and adeptly and placed the body of Margaret Bursley on top of the man. The flames licked higher, engulfing the bodies in their embrace. Angeline had never felt so sick, so ashamed, or so satiated in her entire life.

CHAPTER FOUR

Fog Hollow, Massachusetts, current day

Stacey pulled her Honda up to the Gas 'n' Eats, which was completely blocked off with yellow caution tape and surrounded by ambulances, fire trucks, and police cars. Two police officers were searching Megan's car. She didn't have anything in there that would set off any alarms, but it still felt like a violation of privacy. A group of spectators gathered behind the tape, whispering furiously amongst themselves. These kinds of things didn't happen in Fog Hollow. The last big crime that had taken place was the previous year. Markie Jerczyk had smashed in a few windshields with a bat after his softball team lost in the finals.

"What are you going to tell them?" Stacey asked, scanning the scene.

"The truth, I guess," Megan said.

"What, that some hot psychopath claiming to be a vampire whisked you away from the scene and healed you with her blood?" Stacey smiled sarcastically.

"Well, I can't lie to the police! I just hope they don't think that I'm the nutcase. Do you think they'll send me to the hospital?" Megan winced at the chaotic scene in front of the gas station.

"Definitely. And they should. Your sweater is covered in blood."

"Good point. I really don't want to go to the hospital right now. I'm fine," Megan said, sounding less than confident. She removed her sweater and draped it over her arms, the bloody section pushed up against her stomach. At least the shirt was black, so the evidence was more of a crunchy patch than a glaring bloodstain. "This is surreal. I can't believe this is happening. I'm traumatized over being part of a robbery-turned-murder, I was shot and kidnapped, and now I'm going to have to explain the Bride of Frankenstein to these people."

"Dracula."

"What?" Megan looked at Stacey incredulously.

"Bride of Dracula. You said Frankenstein." Stacey shot her a quick grin and then turned back to the scene at the station.

"Seriously. Does it really matter? Okay, I'm going. Don't leave, they'll probably want to question you too."

Megan closed the door behind her and walked up to the edge of the caution tape. "Excuse me? Officer?"

A tall, broad-shouldered police officer approached her with his hand extended into the "stop" motion. "This is a crime scene, miss. Please back away."

"I was inside when it happened. I saw the whole thing. That's my car," Megan said, pointing to her red Escape. The police officers were still searching her vehicle.

"Hold on, please." The officer walked away and conferred with someone in a suit and tie. The other man nodded and came over to Megan.

"Detective Greg Nolan. State police," he said, offering Megan his hand. He looked to be in his mid to late fifties and had a kind smile. "And you are?"

"Megan Denham."

"We were able to see most of what happened on the surveillance footage, though your face was pretty obscured. We'd love to hear your take on what went on here. Why did you leave the crime scene?"

"I didn't," Megan said, taken aback. She hadn't considered

the fact that she could be in trouble for fleeing. "I was on my knees when the shooter said that I knew what he looked like, so he had no choice but to kill me." Her stomach roiled as she pictured the gun pointed at her. "I heard a loud bang, and the next thing I remember is waking up on the outskirts of the Bullseye parking lot."

Detective Nolan nodded at her, but Megan could see that his facial expression indicated pity. Or maybe disbelief. Either way, anxiety was creeping in.

"How did you get there?"

"I honestly don't know," Megan said, running a hand through her hair. "There was a woman with me when I woke up. She said her name was Angeline. She said that she saved me. And then she was gone." Just saying the words out loud caused embarrassment to heat her cheeks. She sounded like a lunatic, and she was pretty sure the detective viewed her that way too. "I know how it sounds. But it's true."

"On the video, we saw the gunman take aim at you after shooting the clerk, and it did look as if he shot you. Your body jerked forward and we saw what appeared to be blood seeping from your stomach. And then the video went black. Our guys are trying to figure out why that happened and if anything can be recovered. We weren't sure that you made it but figured you must have crawled out of the place or something. We've got some people combing the area. We're waiting for the dogs to arrive so they could pick up your scent. But you don't seem to be hurt?" Detective Nolan raised his eyebrows.

Megan shivered, clutching her sweater between her fists. She took a deep breath and held the sweater up, the bloodstain dried and stiff.

"Jesus. We need to get you to a hospital. Officer Brent here is going to ride with you." He snapped his fingers at a nearby policeman. "Once you're checked out, we'll continue our discussion at the police station where it's a little warmer and a bit more comfortable. Does that sound okay to you?"

He was talking to Megan like a child. She didn't care. "Yes, that sounds fine. I don't really have any noticeable wound from the gunshot. I think it just grazed me."

"Okay, well, let's have a doctor confirm that, shall we? Brent! Get her to Valley, would you? After we know what's going on there, we'll meet up at the Fog Hollow station." Nolan pointed to the ambulance parked just outside of the caution tape.

Brent nodded and gently took Megan by the elbow. She stopped and turned back to Nolan. "The shooter. Is he, uh, dead?"

Nolan's gaze drifted to the truck, and Megan's along with it. She saw the shooter sitting in the driver's seat with his head nestled between the two headrests. His neck was covered in something dark. His mouth was wide open. Megan fought the impulse to scream. For a fleeting moment, she thought she might be sick. Or faint. She turned away quickly.

"Yes," Nolan said. "He's dead. How did you know that?"

"I didn't. That woman, Angeline. She told me he was dead. I don't know how she knew."

Nolan whispered something to Brent. "Okay. Would you be able to describe this woman to a sketch artist?"

Megan swallowed. "I guess so." Brent nudged her toward the ambulance. Megan obliged, walking silently along with him. It felt like a dream. She'd left work just three hours earlier, annoyed with her boss for giving her a weekend assignment. The woes of a real estate appraiser had never felt as insignificant as they did when Megan was loaded into the back of an ambulance, two dead men and swarms of first responders less than fifty feet away.

"Wait," Megan said. "Let me just tell my friend where I'm going." Megan could see Stacey behind the wheel of her car with her arms in the "what's going on" flail. Brent nodded, but followed behind her. Megan felt a little bit like a criminal.

Stacey opened her car door and stood, resting her arms on the roof. "Where are you going?" She looked at Megan and then at Brent, and then at Megan again.

"They're taking me to the hospital after all." Megan shrugged. "It's probably for the best, considering."

"Okay, I'll follow behind the ambulance."

"No, Stace, really. Go home. It's so late, and you know how long emergency room waits can be. I'm fine, I promise."

"Are you sure? Seriously, Meg, I don't mind."

Megan shook her head. "If I need you, I'll give you a call."

Stacey hesitated, but eventually nodded. She sat in her car and watched them until Megan could no longer see her. Megan didn't want Stacey sitting around for hours while they tried to figure out why the woman who was shot wasn't really shot.

After they'd arrived at the hospital and about ten different people had examined and x-rayed Megan's body, the nurse closed the curtain around her bed and Officer Brent let her know he'd be right outside. It was the first moment she'd really had time to think since she'd pulled into the Gas 'n' Eats earlier that night. A lifetime ago. If only she hadn't forgotten her keys on the counter, she'd be in bed, sound asleep, Merlin curled around feet. If only she'd gotten gas that morning, like she'd planned on doing, she wouldn't be wondering if the whole thing with Angeline had been a hallucination. But no, she'd run out of time. Getting coffee had been more important that getting gas. And the coffee had only been mediocre. Not enough sugar.

"Megan Denham?" a doctor asked, pulling aside the curtain. She was an attractive woman of about sixty with her hair pulled back into a French twist. Her brow was furrowed.

"Yes?" Megan said, her voice cracking.

"I'm Dr. Morris. Just looking over your X-ray. According to your report, you aren't sure if you were actually shot or not?" She removed a pair of glasses from her coat pocket and put them on. She held something up to the light.

Megan cleared her throat. "Yes. I know that sounds strange, but I think that maybe I was just grazed and then I…blacked out or something."

"No, you weren't just grazed." She attached the X-ray to the lighted box and pointed. "That's the bullet lodged in your pelvis, near your right sacroiliac joint."

Megan's eyes widened in disbelief. A bright oval object was hovering near her hip. "Are you sure that's a bullet?"

"Well, it certainly appears to be. Is there anything else you think it might be?"

Megan thought for a moment. Of course not. "But it doesn't hurt."

The doctor shook her head, her face scrunched. "Have you ever been shot before? Or had a foreign object pierce your stomach? Have you had any other illnesses that meant you experienced pain or blood loss differently?"

"No," Megan whispered. "Is it possible..." She trailed off with no way to finish that sentence. Angeline flashed through her mind.

"May I examine you?"

"Sure, of course." Megan lay back on the stretcher, her heart racing. It couldn't be a bullet; there was just no way for it to be a bullet. If she'd been shot, it would hurt, it would be bleeding, she'd probably be dead. It had to be some sort of mix-up.

Dr. Morris snapped on a pair of gloves and lifted Megan's hospital gown. She poked at her stomach and pelvis. She pushed down with both sets of fingertips. "You have no pain in this area?"

"No."

"Your sweater had blood on it?"

"It did, yes." Megan held the sweater up for the doctor to see. Dr. Morris shook her head in confusion.

"Well," Dr. Morris said, lifting the blanket over Megan's stomach, "it couldn't be yours. You have no wound or entry point, so the bullet in the X-ray must be from a prior incident."

"But it's not!" Megan said, trying not to sound panicked. "I'd know if I'd ever been shot before, wouldn't I? And the blood on my sweater suggests I was shot, doesn't it?"

"One would think so, yes. And I don't see any evidence of

X-ray on that area in your medical history, so I have nothing to compare it to. Perhaps you could get something from your pediatrician? Maybe they'll have some answers. But no one gets shot and then doesn't have an entry wound, bloody sweater or not." Dr. Morris all but shrugged.

"This is insane. I was in a store when a maniac was shooting at me, the camera showed me collapsing, I have a bullet in my body, and all you can suggest is that I get in touch with my pediatrician? *Really?*" Megan's breaths became rapid and shallow. She tried to push down the terror she was feeling. Falling victim to an anxiety attack wasn't going to help anyone.

"I'm sorry, Ms. Denham. I don't have an explanation for you. You have no open wound, no skin lesions, not even a bruise. A gunshot wound doesn't heal itself that quickly. It simply doesn't. Without an entry point, removing the bullet would do more harm than good, and it isn't in a place that will cause you any further issues. I can have the nurse come in to give you something for your anxiety."

"Can they make you remove the bullet as evidence? It would prove that it came from the robber's gun," Megan said. She touched her side gingerly.

"No, they can't do that. It would violate your Fourth Amendment rights. And I would strongly advise against it if you're considering it for your own benefit. Non-necessary surgery is never a good option. Best of luck."

Megan looked at Dr. Morris incredulously. It was clear that the doctor was at a loss, and while she might have been sympathetic, she had no additional answers.

The nurse came in a short time later, offering Megan a Xanax. She declined, wanting to be able to weed through the memories should could muster with a clear head. Since they found nothing physically wrong with her, aside from the lodged bullet which they were going to leave in place, they discharged her to the care of the Fog Hollow Police Department.

CHAPTER FIVE

"Here you go, Cocoa," Angeline said, placing the small brown Holland Lop back into his cage at Fog Hollow Animal Hospital. It was quiet as usual. The rabbit stayed still for a few minutes so she could pat him. "Who's my sweet little bunny?" Cocoa curled up in his small fleece bed, his floppy ears hanging down to the steel floor below him.

Angeline sighed and sat at the computer. She started typing up her nightly notes when she heard a cat cry, low and loud. She stopped to listen. The cat cried again.

She walked over to the row of cat enclosures and saw the overweight orange tabby had turned over his water bowl. "Ugh, really, Juice? Again?" Angeline grabbed a towel, mopped up the water, and plucked a weighted bowl from the dog cabinet. She filled it halfway and nestled it in the corner. "If you can flip that over, my man, then you are definitely ready to go home. 'Night, pal."

Angeline pulled up PetDesk again and resumed typing. She stopped short when a pang in her stomach nearly doubled her over. "What the hell?" she muttered. Before she could get any more words down, another one hit. After the events earlier that evening, Angeline was determined to concentrate on work and nothing else. How infuriating that woman had been. She'd seemed offended that Angeline had stepped in and saved her. Exactly why she'd saved her was still a bit of a mystery, since she'd been so careful not to get mixed up with anything like that for an awfully long time. But she'd done it, and she didn't regret it. She could have just walked away, pretended like she hadn't seen anything, and found another convenience store nearby. But she'd seen the pleading look in the woman's eyes just before the gunman had pulled the trigger, and she couldn't leave her to die.

The pain felt like a series of needles pricking her abdomen. She stood up, walking around the office to see if it was just a cramp or something like it. Because there was no way it could be that. She hadn't given her nearly enough for it to be that.

Angeline could lie to herself all she wanted, but she'd been around long enough to know exactly what that feeling was.

She slammed her pen down on the desk and shook her head forcefully. She was determined to ignore it. How many times had it happened to her over the years? Three, four? And every time, she vowed that she wouldn't let it happen again. Too much responsibility, too much of a burden. The barriers that she'd carefully constructed around herself didn't mean much if she kept compromising them.

"Just let it go," Angeline said. She sat in her chair again and started entering the notes into Cocoa the bunny's medicine chart. "It's fine. It'll go away."

Satisfied that she might actually be able to ignore it this time, Angeline smiled just a little. Her typing picked up speed as she lost herself in her work. For a few minutes. And then the twinges of pain started up again.

"Damn it," she said, loudly. She pulled up the office contact sheet and traced her finger down the list until she found the number she was looking for.

❖

Megan was surprised to find that the inside of the Fog Hollow Police Department looked nothing like the sterile interrogation rooms on television. There were no stone walls or tables screwed into the floor with handcuffs hanging from them. She was led to a plush leather couch in a room that had a table full of magazines, a small TV hanging on the wall, and a water cooler.

Detective Nolan took a seat on the chair across from her.

"How are you feeling, Megan?"

"Okay," she said. She was lying. She was tired, confused, and annoyed. She really just wanted to go home and pretend like the whole night had been a bad dream.

"I'm sure you're exhausted," Nolan said. At least he was perceptive. "We just need to figure out exactly what went on at the Gas 'n' Eats tonight. As I said, I'm with the State Police, here to help out with the investigation. From what I gather, you don't have many incidents like this around here."

Megan nodded. She wasn't sure what his point was, and frankly, she didn't care.

"Just to confirm, you're thirty-two, you're a real estate appraiser with HomeSure, and you live at forty-seven Shaw Way. Is that correct?"

"Yes."

"Good. Now what were you doing at the Gas 'n' Eats?"

"Getting gas." Megan looked directly at him.

"Right. Your tank was full. Why were you in the store? Pack of gum? Cold soda?"

"I'd forgotten my keys. I usually use my debit card, like everyone else on earth, but I had cash on me. When I went to pay the clerk, I put my keys down to unzip my wallet. I pumped my gas, and then went back for the keys. When I went inside, the shooter was already there, aiming his gun at the clerk." Megan fought back tears at the recall of the clerk's face. His wide eyes, his trembling hands. He was terrified. Minutes later, he was dead. Dead. She could still barely believe those events had really taken place. She swallowed the massive lump in the recesses of her throat.

"Do you need a second?" Nolan asked, leaning forward in his chair.

She took a deep, shaky breath. "No, I'm fine. Anyway, he ordered me to get down on the ground, so I did. The clerk grabbed a shotgun from somewhere behind the counter, but he wasn't quick enough. I don't know why he didn't just give that guy the money and send him on his way." Megan felt tears overflow. "Then I told him I wouldn't say anything if he just let me go, but he shot me anyway. At least that's how I remember it. And the next thing I know, I'm waking up on the grass with a strange woman hovering over me."

Nolan jotted down a few notes. "Angeline, you said? Did she tell you her last name?"

"No."

"We're waiting for the sketch artist to show up, but in the meantime, can you describe her for me?"

Megan shifted, picturing the woman who'd been staring down at her. "She has long dark hair. Wavy. I couldn't tell if it was brown or black, but it's definitely one of the two. I remember her eyes. They were this strange color, like a liquid light brown. Kind of like caramel, maybe. She had on jeans and a hoodie. I think it was red. Or purple. I don't know."

"Okay. And you're sure you don't know her? She didn't look familiar to you at all?"

"No, not at all."

"What did she say to you?"

Megan didn't respond for what felt like minutes. Nolan raised his eyebrows in anticipation.

"Well, she told me that she had saved my life. She said she didn't call for help because there was no time. She didn't say very much."

Nolan chewed on his pen cap. "I'm sure you can acknowledge that this is strange. That you were presumably shot and there's a bullet inside your stomach, but there's no wound. That you disappeared from the crime scene and ended up a mile away with a strange woman who then took off after 'saving' you. The gunman was killed at some point after he shot the clerk, and after he shot you. This doesn't sound like it makes a whole lot of sense, does it?"

Megan just sat there, her head swirling. No, it didn't make sense. It wasn't just Nolan who couldn't wrap his mind around the events of that evening. *Try living it.* "No, it doesn't. But that doesn't make it any less true."

"I'm not saying that," Nolan said, holding up a hand. "I'm just saying that the facts of the case don't line up at the moment. If—*when*—we find your new friend, that may all change. We'd like to send your sweater out to identify the blood on it, just a formality, and we'd also like to take some fingerprints. Are you agreeable to those two things at this time?"

Megan nodded. She didn't see any reason she shouldn't be agreeable. It was her blood, and her fingerprints wouldn't turn up anything that she hadn't already told the detective.

"Great." Nolan waved in a young female officer who collected Megan's sweater, which was folded on the seat beside her, a DNA swab, and some fingerprints. On her way out, Officer Brent stepped in and handed Nolan a manila folder.

Megan shivered from a combination of nerves and the chill in the air. She wanted to ask if they were done, if she could go, but was afraid she was already under suspicion. She didn't want to appear as though she were in a hurry to leave.

"Well, it looks like the clerk was a fifty-three-year-old man named Peter Sampson. Husband and father of two grown children. His family has owned the Gas 'n' Eats for three generations." Nolan paused, shaking his head. "And the gunman was twenty-three-year-old Richard Haim, known to friends as Richie, or Richie Rich to his posse. Small-time criminal trying to make rank in the Boston gang scene. Do either of these names spark anything for you? Any kind of recognition?"

Megan stared at him, trying to digest his words. Two people she had been in the same room with just hours ago were lying on a slab somewhere. She should be on one too, but she wasn't. "No. Neither one."

"Why do you think this woman brought you away from the gas station to save you? Wouldn't it have made more sense to get you some help right then and there?"

More questions she couldn't answer. Megan didn't know how many different ways she could tell the detective that she didn't know. "She told me there wasn't time to call for help. Why she dragged me away from the gas station, I don't know. Maybe she's a criminal. Maybe she's undocumented. I don't know. She told me next time she'd just mind her own business, whatever that means."

"And you've never been shot? Or had any kind of stomach wound before tonight?"

"No. I'm just...me. I have a cat and a best friend, and I work in real estate. My life up until tonight was utterly normal. I don't understand it either."

"What did she say she did to help you? You don't have any bandages or anything like that, right?"

"Right." Megan hesitated. She wasn't sure whether she should tell Nolan what Angeline had said to her. She got the feeling he already thought she was crazy. She didn't see how telling him could possibly help her case. But if she did have a psychopathic killer after her who was under the impression that she was some kind of creature of the night, maybe it would be best to have law enforcement on her side. "She, uh, said that she fed me some of her blood so that I wouldn't die."

Nolan didn't flinch. Megan shifted awkwardly, wondering if she'd be spending the night in a mental hospital instead of in her bedroom. He tented his fingers. "Mm-hmm. She said that to you? Why did she think feeding you her blood would heal you?"

"When I asked her that, she didn't answer me. She said next time she'd just mind her business and then she was gone."

"Did they test you for any communicable diseases at the hospital?"

"They took blood, yes."

Scratching his chin, Nolan looked to the ceiling. "Was she

trying to say that she was a devil worshipper, or a vampire, or some kind of healing angel or something?"

Megan closed her eyes. "I honestly don't know what she was saying. She was gone too quickly for me to ask questions or to follow her. She took off into the trees. She didn't even seem to have a car."

Nolan nodded. "Okay, Megan. As the sole witness to what happened tonight, and...whatever else, please stay close by. I'm sure we'll have more questions, and once we get the results back from our tests, I'll be in touch." He handed her a business card from his jacket pocket. "Do you need a ride home? Your SUV is still a part of the crime scene, so we can't release that to you just yet."

Still in a fog, Megan nodded. "Yes, please."

Nolan called for Brent, who ushered Megan out into his squad car. Megan checked the clock on Brent's dash. Three fifty-five. She watched the trees go by in a blur, trying to remember what life had been like at four o'clock the previous morning.

CHAPTER SIX

Merlin swirled in repeated figure eights through Megan's legs. She tossed her keys on the table and leaned down to stroke him.

"It's been a hell of a night, baby," she said, reveling in his purr. The comfort of home meant release. She fell onto the couch and broke down into sobs.

Everything seemed the same. Her radiators clicked, Merlin had spilled seven or eight pieces of kibble onto the floor near his dish, and her window blind was slightly askew, just as she had left it earlier that afternoon. She had meant to fix it but forgot. How silly a slanted blind seemed after everything that had happened. The thought of getting up and going into her bedroom seemed entirely overwhelming, but Megan didn't want to spend another minute in the clothes that had touched a convenience store floor, dirt, leaves, and shriveled grass. Maybe she would burn them.

She dragged herself to her bedroom, deciding whether or not she had the energy for a shower. She didn't. She threw on a red T-shirt and plaid pants and left her clothes in a pile near her door.

"Don't scream."

Megan screamed, backing up until her closet door abruptly stopped her from going any farther.

"I said *don't* scream."

"What are you doing here? Are you stalking me? The police are on their way over here, you know!" Megan scanned her room for a weapon, but the closest thing she had was a hanger dangling from her treadmill.

Angeline smiled. "No, they're not, but A for effort. And no, I'm not stalking you. But something was bothering you earlier, so I came to see what it was."

"Who *are* you?" Megan asked, her head swimming.

"Angeline. I already told you." She walked farther into the bedroom and looked around.

Megan tried to look at it from a stranger's point of view. It was mostly neat. Megan's bed was made, but she had folded clothes on her dresser that needed to be put away. The walls were a pale yellow with pink accents.

"You don't strike me as a pastels type of girl."

Megan sat gingerly on the edge of her bed, questioning her own sanity. She should be running from the apartment. She should be calling the police. But in theory this woman had saved her, and curiosity got the better of her. "I am begging you, tell me who you are, what you want, and how you got in here. Please."

Angeline seemed to sense that Megan was on the verge of tears. She sighed heavily and leaned against the treadmill. "My name is Angeline Vallencourt, I don't want anything, and I got in through your back slider. I was able to just walk in like I had an open invitation. Your lock snapped like uncooked spaghetti. You should probably have that replaced."

Now she had a broken door to contend with too. "If you don't want anything, then why are you here? In my house? Why were you there tonight? I don't understand. Any of it."

Angeline rolled her neck back and forth. She took off her black overcoat, revealing baby blue scrubs with a Fog Hollow Veterinary Hospital logo above the right breast pocket. Beneath the words was a silhouette of a dog. "Okay. Remember how I told you earlier that I fed you some of my blood to save you? From dying?"

Megan looked away from her awkwardly. "Yes. And that wasn't weird at all."

"I guess I did my job a little too well. Apparently, you drank more than was necessary, so now we're bonded. Blood bond. For real."

Well, that sounded horrifying. "I don't even know what that means. This all sounds like complete nonsense. No offense." The hanger was looking more and more appealing. If Angeline was as delusional as she sounded, Megan feared that she might attack at the slightest provocation. Although her demeanor suggested otherwise.

"None taken." Angeline shrugged. "I'm not usually so open about myself, and I'm sure you can see why. This would be the response ninety-nine-point-nine percent of the time, I'm positive. But I figured what the hell. I'm not in the mood to concoct a story. You seem like a nice enough person. So anyway, when enough of my blood enters your system, it creates a bond between us. When you're upset or panicked or just generally uneasy, I'm going to feel it."

"Come on, that's insane." Megan let out a strangled laugh, unable to make eye contact.

"But true. Why do you think I'm here? You were crying, weren't you?"

Megan looked at the carpet, focusing on the fact that she needed to vacuum. "I was. But anyone could have guessed that. I was nearly killed and there are two people lying in a morgue right now that I saw alive just a few hours ago. Of course I was crying."

"Okay, you can go with that if you want to. That's understandable, of course, but what I was feeling was more of an imminent thing. But I get it. I should probably get back to work anyway. I called in my backup to cover while I checked on you. Since there doesn't seem to be any threat to your life at the moment, I think I'm good."

"Why would you bother? Even if this whole…thing…is true, you don't know me. So what if I'm upset?"

"I have to, especially in the beginning. It's strong, and sort of debilitating. I have an acute sense of what you're feeling. If I don't ease whatever trauma you're experiencing, it becomes mine. Does that make sense?" Angeline asked.

"Sure." Megan rolled her eyes and crossed her arms. "Of course it does."

"It doesn't last forever. As time goes by, the bond gets weaker and weaker, and then it just goes away. That's one of the disadvantages to healing people. It's hard to tell how much is too much. But at least it's temporary."

"Okay." Megan shifted in discomfort. Part of her wanted to escape the lunatic in front of her, but the dissenting part of her was highly intrigued by the sincerity in Angeline's voice.

Without another word, Angeline turned and walked into Megan's kitchen. Shaking her head, Megan got up and followed her. She needed to call the police. At the very least they'd want to talk to her. She dug Nolan's card out of her jeans pocket and shakily dialed his number on her cell. Voice mail. "She's here," she whispered. "Angeline. Hurry." She stuffed the card into her flannel pants and found Angeline in the kitchen with her back turned.

Angeline was standing behind the counter, selecting a knife. She pulled out the butcher knife and turned back toward Megan.

"What are you doing with that?" Megan asked, swallowing hard.

"It's obvious you don't believe me, and I need you to in order for this to be less awkward than it needs to be. So, I'll prove it to you." She held out her arm and began to cut a long slice up the center. She hissed at the contact.

"No!" Megan yelled. She made a move toward her but felt her knees grow weak at the spectacle.

As quickly as the cut opened, it healed. There were no remnants of any wound on Angeline's arm. It was as smooth as it was before she had picked up the knife. "See? And that's how I healed you. Same idea. My blood is magical," she said sarcastically, wiggling her fingers in Megan's direction.

"What are you?" Megan asked. Her voice cracked in a mix of awe and fear.

"I think you know."

"You're a—"

Angeline held her hand up. "We don't have to say it. I've never liked the label. But yes. I have to get going. Your cop friend is going to be here any minute, and I don't really want to deal with that right now."

Megan was about to ask how she knew that but decided it was a fruitless question. She still wasn't sure if she was actually on planet earth, in a terrible dream sequence, or maybe dead. And this was obviously hell.

"Do you live here?"

"In Fog Hollow? Yes."

"How have I never seen you before? It's a small town," Megan said. She swallowed hard.

"Maybe you have. But unless you frequent the vet's office in the overnight hours, it's not much of a mystery. I don't go out all that much. All of these delivery services they have now are a godsend."

Merlin came out from under the bed and sauntered over to Angeline. Her eyes brightened into that honey color that Megan had had such a hard time describing. Angeline picked him up and put her face up to his.

"Oh God, please don't kill my cat!" Megan clamped a hand over her mouth. She'd read enough stories to know that vampires fed on animals as a snack between their human entrées.

Angeline placed Merlin on the floor near his food bowl and turned angrily to Megan. "What do you think I am, some kind of monster? Whatever. Apparently, I'll never learn. If the good detective is looking for me, tell him he'll be hot on my trail somewhere in Transylvania. I'd appreciate it if you didn't tell him where to find me. I'd prefer to continue my quiet existence without law enforcement up my ass."

Angeline walked out the front door and shut it tightly behind her. Megan ran after her, opened the door, and peered down the sidewalk. Nothing. No car, no bicycle, no Angeline. She could hear a siren in the distance growing closer.

Nolan pulled up to her curb and killed his flashers. He saw her standing on the front porch and raised his hands into the "what gives" gesture.

Megan shook her head. "She's gone. She must have heard me call you, though I don't know how. I whispered and I was in my bedroom at the time." She was sort of lying. She was pretty sure she *did* know how; she just didn't want to admit it. Megan grasped on to her last perceived vestiges of sanity with an ironclad grip.

"What was she doing here?" Nolan asked, looking up and down the street. Megan lived on a quiet, tree-lined street with very few cars not in driveways. If there was someone on the street, they'd be easy enough to spot.

"I don't really know," Megan said thoughtfully. She frantically tried to decide if she should tell Nolan the truth or continue to be vague.

"You didn't ask?" He didn't look like he believed her. "Was she here to hurt you? Kill you?"

"Do you want to come in?" Megan asked, holding her door open wide. It was much too chilly to continue the conversation from her front porch. Plus, she had no interest in her neighbors overhearing anything about the undead.

Nolan took a seat at her kitchen table. He played with the fringe of her moss-colored place mat while looking down. Megan offered him something to drink, and when he declined, sat down across from him.

"Look, Megan, if I'm going to help you, you have to be honest with me. I gave you the benefit of the doubt earlier, but I feel like you're either keeping something from me or stringing me along to distract me. Either way, it's an obstruction of justice."

Megan squirmed. "Okay. You want me to tell you? I'll tell

you. She showed up in my bedroom and told me it was because she knew I was upset. By swallowing her blood in that parking lot, it created some kind of weird bond that every time I feel something, she feels it too. She cut her arm and let me watch it heal immediately so she could prove that she'd done what she'd said she'd done. And then she left. I didn't see her drive away, she just seemed to vanish." Megan pursed her lips and shrugged. That was it. He could either believe her, not believe her, arrest her, or commit her. But at least she wasn't waffling between telling him and keeping it a secret anymore.

Nolan just stared at her, much like he had earlier at the station. He laced his fingers together and closed his eyes. "If you were me, Megan, and someone told you that story, how would you react?"

Megan ignored the condescension in his voice. "Honestly? I wouldn't believe them. I barely believe myself, and I was here for it."

"I don't really know how to protect you, if that's even what you need at this point. Tell me something." He leveled his eyes at her. "Did you kill Richie Haim?"

"Of course not! I was *his* victim. You saw that on camera. I didn't even know he was dead until Angeline told me!" Megan felt a bolt of panic shoot through her. They didn't really think she was guilty of killing the shooter, did they? "Did you check for fingerprints?"

"Yes. Everything is being done by the book. But it's not like one of those crime scene shows where every test has results in minutes. Sometimes these things can take days, even weeks. So, if you had something you wanted to tell me, it would be a lot easier to just get it out on the table now instead of waiting."

"I have nothing to tell you that I haven't already," Megan said. She sighed. "I called you, remember? You're not the only one who doesn't understand what's going on. I have as many questions as you do, probably more."

"Did she have an accent? What was she wearing? Anything that might provide some insight into where came from?" Nolan asked.

Megan swallowed. She should just tell Nolan, let him find Angeline, and wash her hands of the whole situation. It would really make things a lot easier, and besides, aside from her life, what did she really owe this woman?

"Scrubs. Blue. Nothing particularly distinctive about them." Dammit. It was her opportunity to come clean, and she couldn't force the words out of her mouth.

He sighed and shook his head. He made a note and looked up toward the ceiling. "Okay. We need to talk to this woman. If she shows up again, please call me. I'll try to get here quicker next time. You don't have any travel plans or anything like that coming up, correct?" Nolan asked. He walked out the front door before turning to face her.

"No, Detective Nolan. I'm not taking off or leaving the country or anything. You don't have to worry about it."

"Good night," he said, jogging down the stairs to his car.

Megan flipped the deadbolt, although the lock on her slider was apparently as strong as uncooked spaghetti. Her house was too quiet. She asked Alexa to play some classical music and turned down her covers. Merlin slept in a ball at the foot of her bed. Megan pulled her comforter up to her chin and stared at the ceiling. She had never been so tired and so wide-awake in her entire life.

CHAPTER SEVEN

Mount Pleasant, South Carolina, 1929

Angeline drew circles in the sand with her toe while Kathryn added a few more sticks to the small fire that separated them. The waves crashed under the starlit sky. Everything was peaceful. Mostly everything.

"I'm so bored. You never want to do anything."

Angeline sighed. "We are doing something. We're enjoying a nice fire on the beach."

Kathryn rolled her eyes. "Somehow I don't think the dark lord or whoever the hell designed us to be ruthless killers envisioned us sitting on a beach sipping iced tea."

"There is no dark lord, Kathryn. We share a blood disease. Nothing more, nothing less. All of those myths are just that— myths. Every library in every city we've been to in the last three years has confirmed the same thing. No one has any idea what we really are. We've become old, stale legends turned into bedtime stories to scare children." Angeline shrugged and continued to mark the sand.

"Ugh, you're such a flat tire. How about we go into Charleston and find a dance hall? I wouldn't mind getting fried on some of those handsome locals." Kathryn raised her eyebrows expectantly.

"No, thanks."

"Or how about, in your case, some of those pretty locals?"

"Knock it off, Kathryn." Angeline stood up and brushed the sand from her blouse. She walked toward the ocean and let the cool water run over her feet. It had been three years, three long years, since she had seen her family, her friends, her home. Kathryn insisted that it would be too dangerous to tell anyone about her transformation. Her own parents might see her as an abomination and have her destroyed. She had no choice but to disappear completely.

At first, Angeline was enthralled by her heightened senses. Lights were brighter, smells were richer, sounds were clearer. She missed the familiarity of Benjamin, but the freedom of her new life allowed her to see that she had settled into what was expected of her. Benjamin was a good man who had treated her with kindness and respect, but the great love of romance novels didn't exist between them. Angeline had never experienced that kind of love with anyone, and she had finally concluded why. She wanted that kind of love with a woman, not a man.

It wasn't that Angeline had never acknowledged those types of feelings within herself. But it simply wasn't an option to outwardly admit that kind of thing. Angeline had always assumed that she had been born with one of the wires crossed in her brain. It was something to power through and ignore, otherwise she'd end up in some sort of facility. Kathryn had shown her that that wasn't the case. In fact, there were many women who shared the same feelings. And there was nothing wrong with that.

In the two hundred years or so that Kathryn had roamed the earth, she'd encountered many different types of people. She'd even had a relationship with a woman once, a duchess, but she'd determined that her preference was men. She'd shared many of her stories with Angeline, and they'd had quite a few laughs over her misadventures. Kathryn's openness and accepting nature was one of the few things that Angeline admired.

What daunted Angeline most was the thought of her parents.

Their devastation, their grief. How were they getting along with the knowledge that their daughter was missing and likely dead? Angeline wasn't the type to just take off without a word, and they knew that. Her mother in particular would never believe that Angeline had run off with another man or had left to start a new life. It wasn't in her bones. If not for the constant threat of her own demise, Angeline would have defied Kathryn years ago to find a way back home.

Angeline closed her eyes as she felt Kathryn's presence sidle up behind her.

"You know, you probably wouldn't be such a wet blanket if you fed a little more often. More energy and less mope." Kathryn twirled a strand of Angeline's hair around her finger.

Angeline pulled away. "I didn't ask for this. I know you wanted a little friend to drag along so you wouldn't have to be alone, but why did you choose me? Maybe I wasn't the picture of happiness and truth, but it was a hell of a lot better than this." It wasn't their first argument in the three years they'd been together, and Angeline was pretty sure it wouldn't be their last.

Kathryn stood back, her eyebrow quirked. "I chose you because I sensed fire within you. I recognized the longing inside you. I thought you wanted to watch the world burn too. Clearly I was mistaken."

"Clearly."

"Plus, you were an easy target. That helped."

"Giving me a choice would have been appreciated. You picked me out the same way a person picks out a dog. Wouldn't you rather have had your partner go along with you willingly?" Angeline could feel the muscles in her gums twitching, threatening to lower her cuspids. She was generally able to keep her anger in check, but she was losing her desire to do so.

Kathryn laughed. "Do you know anyone who would willingly let a person bite their neck and turn them into a vampire? If that person does exist, I assure you, I wouldn't want them tagging along."

"I hate that word and you know it." She cast a glance at the beat-up copy of *Self Mastery Through Conscious Autosuggestion* lying in the sand near their fire pit. Kathryn had mocked her mercilessly for reading it. But it provided her with a way to ground herself. *She can't upset you. She can't upset you. She can't upset you.* Kathryn was pushing her on purpose.

"*Vampire.* Vampire. Sorry, sugar, you're just going to have to accept it. It's who we are. It's who you are. We're the undead. Monsters. Bloodsuckers. Forever and ever and ever."

Before she could stop herself, Angeline pushed Kathryn. Hard. Kathryn flew backward, landing inches from the blazing firepit.

She was back in Angeline's face in an instant. Her fangs were sharp and her eyes flashed with gold. "I wouldn't do that again, little girl. I could snap you in half before you even realized I'd touched you. I've been patient with you. Don't do it again."

Angeline wanted to challenge her but nodded, her jaw clenching. She knew that she was no match for Kathryn. Not only was she considerably older, but she had honed her strength into a lethal weapon.

"I know what you're going through," Kathryn said. She adjusted her jacket as her eyes resumed their regular shade of green. She breathed out heavily. "You're still new to this, so to speak. Three years might seem like a long time, but trust me, eventually it will seem like little more than a day. You'll settle in and embrace it. I struggled for a while, though it was a different time then. Women didn't have the freedoms that we enjoy now. And be thankful you were lucky enough to miss the 'Sinners in the Hands of an Angry God' era. What a drag that sermon was, but people ate it up. My maker wasn't as sympathetic to my plight as I am with yours. I'd go days without seeing him, locked in a crypt with only rats and bugs as companions. He was afraid that I'd expose us."

Angeline contemplated. Accepting a thousand lifetimes of

staying in the shadows and feeding on humans to survive didn't sound possible. *Embracing* it sounded absolutely ludicrous.

"Where is he?"

"Jonathan? Dead." Kathryn's face betrayed no emotions.

"You never talk about him. How'd he die?"

"Well, you know it was only one of three ways. Direct sunlight, fire, or decapitation. And he wasn't sunbathing. It was a long time ago."

Angeline nodded. "Was it you?"

"Me? Of course not. That would be the gravest sin any of us could commit. You don't harm your maker. No matter what." Kathryn looked long and hard at Angeline, who eventually turned away.

"Who did it?"

"Religious zealots. They found his resting spot in St. Lucius's cemetery in Albany. In those days, it was a lot easier to stay hidden in cemeteries. Communities were too small for us to blend in. Usually they would just stake anyone they suspected of vampirism based on all of those old Dracula legends. Which is obviously the preferred method since that only weakens us, like anything through the heart would do, but it doesn't kill us. Our heart doesn't have much of anything to do with living. These guys weren't taking any chances. They staked him, beheaded him, and lit him on fire."

"Wow." Angeline grew quiet, again focusing her attention on the sand beneath her. Sometimes she forgot just how dangerous the world was for her now. Even though her strength had increased tenfold from her previous life, enough determined hunters could easily take her down. It was unusual for Kathryn to be so open. She usually brushed off Angeline's questions and managed to change the subject. Angeline didn't want to let the opportunity slip away.

"When did you finally accept—sorry, embrace—this?" Angeline asked.

Kathryn cocked her head in thought. "I don't know. Early eighteen hundreds, I guess. I finally realized that unless I wanted to be a sad, pale waif for the rest of eternity, I'd better find a way to start enjoying myself."

"Am I the only one you turned?"

"No," Kathryn said, shaking her head. "There have been a few. Some I've grown tired of. Some met an untimely end. It happens."

Angeline scoffed. "How nice to know that I'm in such expendable company."

"I didn't say that. I'm just saying that not everything has a happy ending. I'm sure it will be different with you. We'll be toasting champagne over a bonfire in the year 3035."

The thought sent a swell of nausea through Angeline. "Why are there so few of us? Have you encountered many?"

"Not many. Four, five. We're a very territorial species. Like a dog pissing on the city limits. This is my space, this is yours. No intersection necessary. Or welcome, for that matter. Jonathan told me that every maker must forcefully engrain in their progeny that they are not to just go around making other vampires left and right. I've never turned more than one at a time. It's another one of those unwritten rules we have to follow. I have no way of knowing what others do, but I'm confident that there aren't vast numbers of baby vamps plodding around the world. Up to this point, at least, we've managed to stay undercover. Vampires popping up everywhere would be catastrophic. It's not like it's *never* happened. Go read those books that point to Romania, Moldova. They're more than just fairy tales. As strong as we are, humans are a rascally bunch. They'd find a way to destroy us."

Angeline looked out at the shimmer glinting off the ocean. For a moment, she wondered if she should just walk into the water and keep walking until she reached the center. Surely a shark would eat her, or some unknown species inhabiting the Mariana Trench would make quick work of her, and that would be it. The end.

She sighed, since the fear of drowning, or at least the claustrophobia of being submerged in mile-deep ocean, was still present in her humanity-fueled mind. Kathryn had said those feelings and thoughts would fade over time. Maybe she could find someone to pull the rope of a guillotine. That would be quick and there'd be no time to change her mind.

"Will you please stop contemplating suicide? It's not a good look on you," Kathryn said. She didn't even bother to look over at Angeline. She was slouched in a beach chair with her eyes closed.

"How do you always know what I'm thinking? It's creepy and invasive."

"Because I can read you like a book, Angeline. Some of it's our shared blood, but mostly you're just predictable." Kathryn propped herself up on her elbow. "It will get better. I promise."

Angeline lay back on the sand, her eyes wide open, staring up at the stars. Maybe they'd both just fall asleep and daylight would turn them into a pile of ash. She shook the thought from her head and focused on the sky. Her despair was real. But so was her hope. There had to be a flicker of light somewhere in the darkness. Angeline just needed to find it.

Chapter Eight

Fog Hollow, Massachusetts, current day

Megan sat on Stacey's couch sipping her lemonade while Stacey answered the door for the pizza deliverer. The smell made her stomach grumble.

"I didn't realize how hungry I was," Megan said, selecting one of the biggest slices and sliding it onto a paper plate. "I slept for like twenty-seven hours."

"Carlos was fine with it?" Stacey asked, biting into her pizza.

"Yeah, he was great. Told me to take the rest of the week off. He's going to cover my appointments for me." Carlos was the owner of HomeSure Appraisal Company, and Megan had been working for him for nearly five years. She enjoyed their relationship. It was a perfect mix of professionalism, laughter, and nonsensical arguments.

"Good. Take the time. You need it." Stacey checked her cell phone. "Have you talked to your aunt yet?"

Megan nodded. "Yes, I told her everything. Well, mostly everything. I left out the whole Angeline part of the story. She freaked out when I told her I'd been shot, but she had calmed down by the end of the conversation. I told her it just grazed me and that I was fine. She asked if I wanted her to come down from Laconia, but I told her absolutely not. Her arthritis has been killing her."

Aunt Susie had been her guardian for as long as Megan could remember. Her mother had taken off when she was just a baby. She was young and scared and decided that Megan would be better off with someone who was stable and loving and actually wanted to be a parent. She was probably right. Aunt Susie, who was technically her great-aunt, had been a wonderful caregiver, and Megan loved her with everything she had. She'd met her mother a few times over the years, and they'd been friendly, but Megan knew in her heart that Aunt Susie was her real mother. And she was perfectly okay with that. She was grateful to her biological mother for giving her the chance to be loved by such a kindhearted woman.

Stacey looked at her phone. "Kristen's on her way home."

"Did you tell her about Angeline?"

Stacey looked guilty. "Of course I did! You didn't tell me not to."

Megan closed her eyes. She wasn't upset that Stacey had told her girlfriend about Angeline, but she didn't look forward to the pitiful glances or questions she was sure would follow. Megan assumed everyone just thought she was whacked.

"No, it's fine. What did she say?"

Stacey kept eating. "She's super sad for the clerk's family. I guess her mom knows his wife. It's awful. The whole Angeline thing, on the other hand...she's kind of intrigued by it."

Megan nearly choked on her pizza. "In what way?"

"I think she sort of believes her! I told her everything, the healing deal, the showing up at your house, the arm thing. None of it makes sense at face value, but if she *is* telling the truth, then it all clicks into place."

"Stacey, she *is* telling the truth. I know it's insane, and I know any rational person wouldn't believe it. But I saw it. There's no way someone could do that to their arm and have it heal like that. It's just not possible. Have you ever heard of anything like that? Some medical marvel or something?" Megan sighed, still trying to convince herself that her eyes might have deceived her.

"No." Stacey pursed her lips. "But what about like, an illusionist? You know, you see those people on TV all the time who levitate or show up with someone else's tattoo on their back. It's all just sleight of hand and mind tricks."

The thought had crossed Megan's mind, but motive was lacking. She had never met Angeline before the night at the gas station. Why would a random person feel the need to gaslight her after removing her from the scene of the crime? There was no rational reason Megan could come up with that made sense. *Not that rational reason is my strong point these days.* Megan shook her head.

"I don't think so. I mean, I guess it's possible, but *why*? Maybe I should go talk to her." Megan bit her bottom lip.

"Do you know where she lives?"

"No, but I know where she works." Megan pointed to the logo on her shirt. "She was wearing those scrubs, remember?"

"You really think she works there?" Stacey asked.

The door flew open and Kristen went running over to Megan. She swept her into a hug. "I can't even believe what you went through. You must be so traumatized."

Megan smiled into Kristen's thick blond hair, which was quickly smothering her. "I'm okay. Lucky to be alive."

Kristen held her at arm's length. "Seriously. Thankfully, that vampire swooped in and killed that dude."

Megan's jaw fell. It sounded even more unrealistic hearing it from someone else's mouth. "I don't know that she killed him. Or that she's a vampire. Maybe she's just really off. None of it makes sense."

Kristen raised her eyebrow skeptically. When Megan looked to Stacey for help, Stacey concentrated even harder on her slice of pizza.

"From what Stacey's told me, it seems pretty cut and dried. She saved you, she told you how, she proved it. What's not to get?" Kristen nudged Stacey over on the couch with her hip and grabbed a slice.

Megan sat back down on the couch in disbelief. "How are you so okay with this? You just believe it? No questions asked? Vampires aren't real!"

"I think your lady vamp would beg to differ. Who says they're not real? There's been tons of documented cases of unsolved murders, people doing things under the influence of something they can't remember, holy water turning people to ash." Kristen shrugged.

"You made that up."

"Okay, I made the last thing up. But the rest of it is totally true, so I don't see any reason to doubt her. Not based on what I know. And there are still tons of things we don't know about the world. People are still discovering new species all the time. Maybe she's just one that's gone underground, so to speak. Did you try to throw garlic at her or show her a mirror?" Kristen asked.

"I can't even believe this is a real conversation," Megan said. "No, I didn't do any of those things. I've been waffling between thinking that I'm insane, thinking that I misunderstood, and thinking that I can be on the cover of *Time* magazine for finally proving the existence of the supernatural."

"It's probably a combination of all three." Stacey swallowed a slug of beer and smiled.

"Well, I think you should confront her. If you know where she is, why not go to *her* this time? Stacey told me that you think she works at the vet's office?" Kristen asked.

"I think. But maybe she stole those scrubs from some unsuspecting victim. I was just talking to Stacey about that. I feel like I should go talk to her, but I don't know. It's a long shot, to be honest," Megan said.

"Let's go," Kristen said, standing. She brushed the pizza crumbs off of her jeans.

"Go where?"

Kristen rolled her eyes. "To the vet office!"

Megan's eyes widened. "Why?"

"Don't you want to know the truth?"

"I guess so, but if she is some sort of deranged serial killer, do you think seeking her out is the best idea? She might see me and go berserk and stab me in the throat. I don't think it's worth the risk." Megan stayed seated on the couch and took another sip of lemonade.

"Come on," Stacey said, looking at Kristen. Kristen was clearly looking for backup. "If you have any inclination that things are about to go bad, we'll swoop in and rescue you. Or we can just go in with you. But since she only told you about this vampire stuff, she might not appreciate me and Kristen showing up too. She'll glamour us to forget everything and we'll be walking zombies for the rest of our lives." She paused. "You know what, Kris? Maybe Megan's right."

"You two are such wimps. Don't you think she would have killed Megan by now if she intended to do so? She's had the opportunity, and both times she let her go. I don't think she's out for blood. So to speak."

Megan sighed. Kristen was nothing if not persistent. "Fine. Follow behind me in case you need a quick getaway. When you hear my bloodcurdling scream, get the hell out of there."

Minutes later, Megan pulled out of Stacey's driveway with the other two in tow. The police department had released her Escape back to her earlier that morning, since nothing of interest was found in the vehicle. Not that she had expected there to be. Megan was surprised the blood results hadn't come back yet. There was a tiny part of her that was nervous about the findings, even though she knew she didn't have anything to do with the gunman's murder. She'd seen so many shows where the innocent victim was caught in the crosshairs and had become the prime suspect. Disappearing from the crime scene certainly couldn't have helped.

They pulled into the Fog Hollow Animal Hospital parking lot, where Megan checked the clock on her dash. Seven fifty-three. A quick scan of their website showed they were open until eight p.m. on Thursday nights, so she still had a few minutes to check things out. Even if Angeline did work there, there was no guarantee she was working on that particular day.

Megan shot a look at Stacey and Kristen, who looked giddy. They were shooing her toward the door. Stacey put down her window. "We're right here if you need us! There are still some employees inside. I see someone at the counter."

"Yeah, thanks," Megan mumbled. She took a deep breath and ran a hand through her hair. There was no reason to be there, other than to satisfy her curiosity. And her friends' curiosity, for that matter. It was stupid.

She was about to turn around and head back to her car when the door opened. A young woman walked out, her pug bounding behind her. The dog ran over to Megan's ankle and snorted at her. She smiled and gave him a quick pat before pulling it together and entering the vet's office.

"We're just about to close," the woman behind the counter said, locking her cabinets. "What can I do for you?"

"Just a quick question. Is Angeline working today?" Megan's heartbeat quickened.

The woman frowned. "Who?"

For some strange reason, Megan felt the tiniest hint of disappointment envelope her. "Oh, I must have the wrong clinic. Sorry about that." She smiled and turned toward the door.

"Oh, wait a minute. I just started here last week and I don't know everyone's names yet. Yes, she's the overnight tech. Her shift starts in five minutes," the woman said, checking a schedule laid out on the desk in front of her. "If you want to leave your name, I'll have her give you a call."

"No need." The door chime rang as someone came in. "How can I help you?"

Megan turned to find Angeline standing there, her head cocked with an amused look on her face.

"Hi," Megan said, her voice thick. "I wanted to speak to you about, um, my cat."

Angeline nodded. "Sure. I remember Merlin. Sweet guy. Greta, I'm going to take Megan out back with me while I set up for the night. Let me know if you need anything on your way out."

Greta nodded, barely looking up from her open purse. She looked like she'd checked out long before the clock struck eight.

Megan followed Angeline into the back room amid the sounds of barking and meows and possibly even a tweet or two. It was hard to tell. She lifted her phone and saw she had four text messages from Stacey.

Is she there?
HELLO?
Should we come in?
Are you alive??? WTF!?

Megan smiled. It was a good thing she hadn't needed them up to this point, or she'd very obviously be dead.

She's here. Ok for now. Don't come in.

Megan slid her phone into the back pocket of her jeans as Angeline hung her jacket up on a hook behind a small computer workstation. Angeline leaned against the desk and crossed her arms.

"So?" she asked.

"So what?"

"What are you doing here?"

Megan looked around the room. "I honestly don't know. After our last…encounter…I felt like maybe I should, I don't know, get in touch?" *God, I sound stupid.*

Angeline nodded, the same look of amusement playing on her lips. "Well, here I am. I haven't been pulled to you since that first night, so things are going well enough, I presume?"

"Well enough, I guess. I mean, I was nearly killed, and two men died less than a week ago. Otherwise, totally fine."

"Touché. Did you just come here to watch me work, or was there was something you wanted to talk about?" Angeline walked into the hallway, readying a syringe on a sterile countertop.

"What's that for?" Megan asked, slightly uneasy.

"Jacques. Diabetic poodle," Angeline said, nodding to a large crate against the wall. The white poodle cocked his head when he heard his name.

"I have to ask. Do you work here so you can, you know, drink blood without anyone knowing?" Megan swallowed hard, her stomach flip-flopping.

Angeline laughed as she flicked the syringe to remove the air. "Of course not. Why do you keep implying I'm some sort of animal killer?"

Megan thought for a minute. Wasn't that sort of a thing in vampire lore? When humans were scarce, or the vampire didn't want to feed on humans, they went for animals? Megan was pretty sure she'd seen that more than once. "I thought that's what vam—you people did."

"Well, maybe some do, but I certainly don't. I work here because I prefer the company of animals to about ninety-nine percent of people. *You* people," Angeline said. "Plus, it's an overnight shift, which is helpful."

"Oh, an overnight shift. So you don't have to go outside in the…" Megan trailed off. She felt more than a little uncomfortable discussing those things. The same thoughts, again and again. Nutty? A marvel?

"Okay, you're obviously weirded out by this whole thing, which hey, I can't blame you. Why don't you just ask me whatever questions you have so that we can have a conversation that doesn't revolve around *this*," Angeline said, flicking her hands toward herself. "Let me go take care of the cats," she looked at her clipboard, "and Ginny the gerbil, and I'll be right back. Have a seat."

Megan watched as Angeline tied her hair up into a messy ponytail and stuck a pen behind her ear. Aside from the fanged elephant in the room, Angeline was really, *really* attractive. Megan cleared her throat, trying to focus on the matter at hand.

Megan sat at the desk Angeline had left her at, presumably

her own. There was a framed photo of a lake, or maybe a river, and a few greeting cards thanking Angeline for her kindness and warmth toward Fluffy and Spot. Megan shot off a quick text to Stacey.

Megan: *Are you still here?*

Stacey: *Yes, are you ok?*

Megan: *Yes, I'm fine. She's doing her rounds and then we're going to talk. I think you can leave. I don't think she'll hurt me.*

Stacey: *Not leaving. We'll go across the street and grab some fries, but we'll be back.*

Megan: *Ok thx*

She slid her phone back into her pocket as Angeline came around the corner. She grabbed an armless office chair from a nearby desk and sat on it, backward. She checked her watch. "I'm good for about thirty minutes, and then I need to take our guests for their pee breaks. So, ask away."

Megan caught herself looking intently at Angeline's eyes. They were mesmerizing. She squinted hard and pinched the bridge of her nose. "Okay. Anything?"

"Anything."

"Did you kill that guy at the gas station? The shooter?"

"Yes."

Megan looked down. She didn't know how to feel about that. "Why?"

Angeline looked taken aback. "Why? Because he had just shot you, and I needed to focus on you. If I hadn't dealt with him, he could have shot me, or worse, while I was trying to get you out of there. And he was a bad guy."

"So you can die from a bullet wound?"

Angeline shook her head. "No, but it weakens me. Until I can get the bullet out."

"You've been shot before?"

"Sure, many times."

Megan nodded. Perfectly normal. "How did you do it?"

"I slit his throat."

"Mm-hmm." Megan shifted uncomfortably. Maybe she didn't want to know these things.

Angeline seemed to sense her discomfort. "It's not something I find enjoyment in doing. You were on the ground, but he was right there. If he had seen that you weren't dead, he might have shot you again, and I wouldn't have been able to save you from a bullet to the head."

"What were you doing there? At the gas station?"

"I needed some paper towels and I forgot to stop before I got to work. I left my car here, at the clinic, and walked over to the Gas 'n' Eats before my shift started. I didn't feel like stopping after work. When I got there, that guy still had his gun pointed at you." Angeline tucked a piece of hair behind her ear.

"Did you, you know, drink his blood?" Megan asked, not meeting Angeline's eyes. She was certain a more bizarre question had never passed her lips.

"I didn't. There wasn't time. I had to take care of you before I did anything else. I'm not sure if you realize just how badly you were wounded."

Angeline had a point. Megan knew there was bullet inside her, but was she really that close to death? The thought sent a shiver up her spine.

"Does garlic burn your skin?"

"No."

"Do you have a reflection?"

"Yes."

"What does blood taste like?"

"Well," Angeline said. She paused. "It's hard to describe. It's not about the taste, really. You don't taste much. It's more like a drug. Euphoric, kind of. Once it starts coursing down your throat, it feels like heaven on earth."

"Do crosses make you shrivel up and die?"

Angeline laughed. "No! You really need to read something other than Bram Stoker. I don't sleep in a coffin either. Shocker, I know."

"Can you go out during the day?"

"That one, unfortunately, holds some truth. It's not quite like television, where if I walk out in the sun I'll burst into flames, but it does weaken me quite a bit. It feels like I'm suffering from a strong sunburn after just a few minutes. After an hour or so, I'd start to burn from the inside out. It would eventually kill me. I try to avoid sunlight as much as possible." Angeline checked her watch. She smiled at Megan. "Anything else?"

Megan breathed in deeply. "Why aren't you killing me? Why aren't you trying to drink my blood, if that's what you do to people?"

"I'm not a monster, Megan. I was in the wrong place at the wrong time, a very long time ago, and I ended up with an inexplicable blood disorder that leaves me so vitamin deficient that I have to replace my defective blood with the blood of others. I don't want to tear people apart or set villages on fire while I pillage them. It's not like that. I take what I need, discreetly, and I do everything possible never to kill anyone. I haven't in a very long time."

Angeline had a look of sadness in her eyes that made Megan's heart flutter. "That's what it is, really? A blood disorder?"

Angeline shrugged. "I don't know that for a fact, but it's the best explanation that I can come up with. I've read so many books over the years, researched as much as I could possibly find, but I've never come up with any real answers. I know that I'm *not* the devil's bride or anything weird like that. And I like my description the best."

Megan shifted, fighting the urge to reach out and touch Angeline's long brown hair. She was pretty sure it would be soft to the touch, but she still wanted to feel it for herself. "Are you immortal?"

"That's the one part of this I can't seem to rationalize. I don't know if I'm immortal, but I do know that I don't age. I look the same as I did when I was turned, ninety years ago."

Megan gasped. "*Ninety* years ago?"

"Give or take a few."

"How old were you?"

"Twenty-six."

For a brief moment, Megan had forgotten how ludicrous the conversation sounded. Everything Angeline was saying sounded like the truth, but it was all too unrealistic for Megan's logic to accept.

"And you believe that all of this is true?" Megan said before she could bite the words back. Obviously, Angeline believed it was true. That was one thing she didn't question. Angeline might have been living in a fantasy world, but she wasn't lying.

Angeline stiffened and stood up straight. "You don't? Then what are you still doing here?"

Megan reached out and put her hand on Angeline's arm, expecting it to be cold or slimy, or something. It wasn't. It was warm and the connection sent a tingle throughout her body. Angeline pulled quickly away.

"I'm sorry, I shouldn't have said that. But I mean, you have to cut me some slack here. This isn't the kind of thing that a person can just accept and say, 'Oh, okay, you're a vampire, wanna play checkers and then turn into bats?' It's not that easy."

"I get it. It's just exhausting to go through this every time. You wonder why we don't come out to people, well, this is why. That, and the innate need to stake us through the heart, of course." Angeline still looked annoyed, but she seemed to have softened up a bit.

"Is that true? Stakes through the heart is the only thing that can kill you?"

"No. It actually doesn't kill us. It hurts, and if it isn't removed will put us into something like a coma. But extended exposure to sunlight, decapitation, and fire will all do the trick. A quick burn will heal, but there's no coming back from a pile of ash. Listen, I have to go walk some dogs. I know this was a lot to take in, so if you want to head out, I won't be offended. I do ask that you not tell anyone where I work. I enjoy this job, and having to leave because of a lynch mob would really suck." Angeline grabbed a few harnesses off of a hook in the hallway.

Warmth crept up Megan's face. "Well, actually—"

"I know your friends in the parking lot know. I'm talking about your detective buddy. You didn't tell him where to find me. Why?"

"You asked me not to." Megan didn't elaborate and Angeline didn't push. She was glad Angeline didn't question her further. She wasn't sure she'd have been able to answer.

"If you want me to try to talk to him, I will. I know it's unfair that you're in this position with the police because of me." Angeline tucked a strand of hair behind her ear and adjusted a tack on the bulletin board.

"Do you really think that's a good idea?" Megan couldn't imagine that anything Angeline could tell the detective would make him back off. There weren't many scenarios where Angeline wouldn't end up in trouble.

"Not entirely, but I also don't want it to be solely your burden."

"No," Megan said, sure of her answer. "I can handle it. If I run into trouble and need you to bail me out, I'll let you know. But for now, I'll just keep being vague, I guess."

"Thank you, Megan," Angeline said, making direct eye contact. "Now, I assume your friends aren't going to try to drown me in holy water?" Angeline nodded toward the parking lot.

"No, of course not. Does that actually work?"

Angeline rolled her eyes. "Good night, Megan. Try not to have any intense bouts of emotion over the next few weeks, so our bond can weaken naturally, and I won't have to come check on you every time you watch *Steel Magnolias*."

Megan's eyes widened. "How did you know I love that movie?"

Angeline chuckled. "Just a guess. Now go, the pups are crossing their paws waiting for me."

"Will I see you again?" Megan asked, surprising herself. She was afraid of Angeline, in the abstract sense of the word at least, but her allure was just as strong. She'd be lying if she said she wasn't attracted to her. But she drank blood. And was a hundred. And burned to death if she stayed in the sun too long.

"What's going on there? I literally just said to watch the emotion," Angeline said, wiggling her fingers toward Megan's stomach. She smiled warmly.

"Oh, nothing. Sorry. I'm hungry, that's all."

"Sure, okay. And yes, we'll probably run into each other again at some point."

Megan nodded and started toward the exit.

"Megan?" Angeline called.

"Yeah?"

"You don't have to be afraid of me. I won't hurt you."

"I know." Megan turned and walked out into the parking lot, the door slamming shut behind her. It was true. In some deep part of her psyche, she knew Angeline wouldn't hurt her. Mixed emotions coursed through her, most of which she didn't understand. There was a certain undeniable allure to the unknown, which Angeline definitely was. If asked directly she might deny it, but Megan believed that Angeline was telling the truth. She decided she might need a few more means of proof, but Angeline seemed open enough to oblige.

Megan waved to Stacey and Kristen, who were seemingly passed out in the front seats of Stacey's car. Neither of them waved back, so Megan assumed they were napping. She laughed and shook her head. Good thing she wasn't in danger or else she'd probably be toast. Still, she was heartened by their loyalty. She knocked on Stacey's window.

"What!" Stacey yelled, startling awake.

"Nothing, it's me! I just wanted to tell you that you can go now. Thank you for staying."

"How did it go?" Stacey asked, putting her window all the way down.

"Fine. Good."

"That's it?"

Megan yawned, more for effect than anything else. "I'm super tired, but I'll fill you in on everything tomorrow. I promise."

"You suck."

Megan tried to come up with a campy vampire-suck joke but heard something in the distance. She turned to see Angeline walking a beagle next to the building, a scoop in one hand and a leash in the other. Megan decided to forgo the joke and smiled instead.

"Call you tomorrow." She watched Stacey drive off. Before she got into her own car, she had the urge to see Angeline again. Megan walked quietly over to the fence, where Angeline was adjusting a beagle's collar.

"Back so soon?" she asked, looking up at Megan.

"Yeah. Do you want to grab a cup of coffee? In the morning maybe?" Megan asked. She had no idea what the hell she was doing. But it felt right.

"Well, the morning might be a little difficult."

"Oh, I know. I meant really, really early. Maisy's opens at four a.m." Megan swallowed hard. Maybe Angeline didn't want to have coffee with her. It was entirely possible that she just wanted to pretend like the incident at the gas station had never happened and move on with her life. The blood bond posed a small problem with that notion, but that didn't mean that she wanted to see Megan socially.

"That sounds great. Are you normally up that early?"

Angeline smiled broadly. Megan felt the words catch in her throat. Striking didn't even cover it.

"Yes! Actually, no, never. But I can set my alarm," Megan said. *Do I always need to sound like a complete idiot?*

"If you're sure you're okay with waking up before the rooster crows, then I would love to. Maisy's has an amazing herbal tea selection too," Angeline said.

"Perfect. I'll see you then."

Megan gave a small wave and then headed back to her car. Alone, she laughed at her own audacity. She knew she'd better get home quickly and try to fall asleep fast. Merlin would wonder if she'd lost her mind.

CHAPTER NINE

Megan sat across from Detective Nolan, nervously chewing on her thumbnail. He'd called her in to the station without any explanation as to why he needed to see her in person. She knew that she'd had nothing to do with the shooter's death, so there wasn't a whole lot of reason to worry. But this time, she knew what had happened to him. Neither she nor Angeline had brought it up again at Maisy's. The conversation had been light and easy, mostly about the animals Angeline treated and how they'd managed to never run into each other in such a small town. Nothing about the supernatural or the fact that Megan was pleased to see that Angeline drank things other than blood. They finished with plenty of time for Angeline to get home before the daylight broke over the hills. They'd left it with another "see you around," but this time Megan believed it. She prayed that the police didn't want to hook her up to a lie detector.

"Coffee?" Nolan asked. He seemed distracted, pulling files together on the table in front of them.

"No, thank you. I'm good."

He nodded. "Well, I wish I was calling you here under better circumstances."

Megan's heart rate quickened.

"We finally got our results back, and I think," he turned to look at the calendar, "seven days is a pretty good turnaround time. Unfortunately, we don't have much more information than we did the night of the robbery. None of your prints match the inside of Haim's car or the prints on his body. The blood on your sweater is, in fact, yours. Which leads us to a whole slew of other questions that we can't answer. Has the vampire lady shown up again?" Nolan leaned back in his chair and crossed his arms over his chest.

"No," Megan lied. She hoped her eyes weren't betraying her. She held Nolan's gaze for as long as possible without appearing to challenge him. "She showed up that night, and that was it."

"And you still stand by your story that she is a supernatural being that filleted her own arm open, only to immediately heal it in front of you?" Nolan narrowed his eyes at her.

Shit. Megan didn't know what to say. Maybe if she told him that she was hallucinating that night, he'd accept it and move on from her. And Angeline. But if she went that route, chances were good that he wouldn't believe anything that came out of her mouth from that point forward. *Shit.*

"I don't know," she said slowly. "That's what I think I saw, yes. But the more time that passes, the more outrageous it all seems." Megan swallowed hard. *Good. Keep it vague.*

Nolan let out an exaggerated sigh. "Once the tech guys got in there, there was no surprise that the camera had stopped working. Standard analog camera hooked up to a digital recorder. Seems that the transmission cable had been pulled right out of the box. Ripped, actually, since the little metal thing on the end was still stuck in the slot on the recorder. Doesn't make a lot of sense. I suppose it could have been the clerk, Sampson, when he fell from the gunshot. Maybe his elbow got caught on the wire or something like that." Nolan furiously tapped a pen on the table. "Doesn't seem all that plausible, though. He would have had to have fallen so precisely for that to happen that it seems like a one in a million chance. Funny how it went black just after you fell to the ground."

Megan raised her eyebrows. "Well, you know it wasn't me. I'm pretty sure I was on the ground with a bullet in me by then."

Nolan nodded. "Yep. You were. I never said it was you. But something isn't fitting here, Megan. We have your gunshot wound without a wound. We have you missing from the crime scene when the first responders arrive. We have you telling me that a vampire rescued you and then disappeared into thin air. Except, of course, when she showed up at your house to prove herself to you. Was there someone else there with you, Megan?"

Megan shifted in her seat, dread swirling in her stomach. "Where?"

"At the gas station that night."

"You mean besides Peter Sampson and Richie Haim?"

"Yes."

"No! Who else would have been there? Detective, I'm not sure what you're trying to get at, but if you're implying that I had something to do with the robbery, you couldn't be more wrong." Megan tried to stave off the tears that were forming in her eyes. "Didn't you find the money that he stole?"

"We did. It was on the floor near the paper towels."

"Then what motive would I even have? This is crazy!" Megan sounded hysterical, but she couldn't stop herself. The thought of going to prison for a crime she didn't commit, and was a victim of, was too much for her to digest.

"I don't know!" Nolan slammed his fist on the table, shaking it from side to side. It was the first time Megan had seen him lose his cool. She inched back in her chair.

He held a hand up. "I'm sorry. You can go. But I need you to remember that anything you don't tell me about that night, or anything relevant that happened after, is an obstruction of justice. That's a felony offense that can carry up to ten years with it. I just want you to remember that."

Unmoved by Nolan's blatant threat, Megan snatched her purse off the back of the chair and exited the room without acknowledging him. She stormed out of the police station and sat behind the wheel of her Escape for a minute, wondering how the hell she had ended up here. A light knock at her window nearly caused her to scream.

"You okay?"

Angeline stood there with dark sunglasses, a winter cap, and a parka obscuring her small frame, even though it was nearly sixty degrees. She kept her head down.

Megan was about to ask her how she knew she was there, but then decided that asking her every time would grow tiresome quickly. Just because she didn't necessarily want to believe how Angeline knew where she was, she'd given her the explanation more than once. "Yes, I'm fine. I think he suspects I had something to do with it. The robbery, the deaths, I don't even know. Thanks to you saving me, there are questions they don't have answers to, and they seem to think I'm lying. Sorry if I 'called' you here." Megan wasn't sure if she should thank her for coming or ask her to get in. So she did neither.

"Don't be. I can't stay out here, though," Angeline said, nodding toward the fading sun. It was just after five, but the sun hadn't gone below the horizon yet. "We can talk about it later, if you want." She slid a folded-up piece of paper into the palm of Megan's hand. Megan clutched Angeline's fingers for the briefest of seconds. Angeline squeezed back and turned to get back into the ink-black Mustang awaiting her. Predictable, but still sexy.

Megan watched as she sped away, wondering why she didn't use her super-speed or whatever power it was that vampires supposedly possessed. Angeline had scrawled her phone number on the sticky note. Her handwriting was small and neat and looked like something out of an old diary. Megan smirked and shook her head. She started her engine and decided she needed a night out. A night without policemen, or vampires, or anything else that made her feel like she was losing her mind.

❖

Pantsuit, the only women's bar in a forty-mile radius, was hopping for a Thursday night. When Megan had called Stacey to ask if she felt like going out, Stacey was only too happy to oblige. Clubs weren't really Megan's scene, or hadn't been since her early twenties anyway. In the late nineties and early two thousands, clubs were the premier place to meet other gay women, so Megan had sucked up her disgust of loud, pulsing music and bathroom lines that stretched as far as the eye could see in order to hang out with like-minded people. A defunct nightclub in Boston was where she had met Stacey all those years ago, and for that she'd be forever grateful.

Kristen and Stacey were standing outside the entrance when Megan walked up the faux red carpet toward the door. Stacey was wearing a tank top and skinny jeans while Kristen had on a bulky sweater and leggings with knee-high boots laced all the way up. It was no surprise that Stacey was shivering, and her lips were a pretty shade of blue.

"You made it!" Kristen yelled, giving Megan a half-hug. "We haven't been out in *forever*. I'm so glad you wanted to do this."

"Yeah, me too," Stacey said, her body trembling. "Can we go in?"

"You had nothing else you could've worn?" Megan asked, rubbing Stacey's tricep vigorously. It was frigid.

"It's been a while, okay? Isn't this the kind of thing we used to wear when we went out?"

"Well, yes, when we went out in June. Not when it was forty degrees outside. You're going to need a shot of whiskey to thaw you out," Megan said.

Not much had changed over the last twenty or so years. The dark purple walls were lined with fluorescent 3-D beer advertisements, flyers for upcoming events, and twinkling Christmas lights. The mahogany bar was full of women, some hoping to meet Ms. Right, some hoping to meet Ms. Right Now, and some were just enjoying the atmosphere with friends. Two pool tables in the room off to the right had quarters piled high, where a smaller bar was decorated with a tropical theme. The dance floor in the main area was throbbing with strobe lights and a techno dance song that Megan was fairly sure would cause one hell of a headache later on that night.

"Come on, let's go over there," Stacey shouted over the noise, pointing to the side room with the pool tables. The music was somewhat muted on that side of the club, but Megan could still feel the pulsing within her temples.

Kristen ordered them a round of margaritas and found a small table in back. Megan looked down at her jeans and V-neck sweater and wondered if the younger crowd saw her as the sweet aunt dropping off oatmeal cookies for the party. She rolled her eyes at her own absurdity.

"So why did you want to come here tonight?" Stacey asked, squeezing her lime.

Megan shrugged. "I don't know, really. I just figured it would take my mind off everything. I wanted to feel normal for a night. You know, relax without having to think too much. I'm rethinking the whole club thing, though. Maybe I should have suggested a movie or a ceramics class."

"Oh, stop," Kristen said. "This is fun. Do you want to go dance?"

"Maybe later," Megan said. *Maybe never.*

Stacey moved her head to the rhythm of the music. "Do you think you've seen the last of her?" she asked in a low voice when Kristen excused herself to the ladies' room.

Megan didn't have to ask who Stacey was talking about. "I don't know. I have these weird feelings about her, Stace. Like, I'm super attracted to her, which is weird in and of itself, and I sort of want to act on it. She makes me feel all mushy inside," Megan said with a laugh. "I'm usually so pragmatic about this sort of thing. You remember, I made a fucking pro and con list before I started seeing Jessica! And right now, there are about four hundred cons to two or three pros. I don't really know her. But I like Angeline, and it's really confusing me."

"What if she's just crazy?" Stacey asked, suddenly looking uncomfortable. Megan noticed her looking around the room.

"I don't think she is. I guess I could be wrong, but my gut is telling me I'm not. I think she might be the real deal."

"What is it about her that makes you interested in her, like *that*? I get having a thing for bad girls, but isn't this maybe a step too far? What if she snaps? Or if she really is just unbalanced and escaped from somewhere?" Stacey asked, scanning the room again.

"What are you looking at? I don't know. She feels like some dark savior out of a romance novel, and as unhealthy as that may be, I find it…intriguing. I didn't say it was smart." Megan shrugged.

"Okay," Kristen said, returning from the restroom and taking her seat next to Stacey. She looked toward the small bar and raised her eyebrows. "I think that girl over there is checking you out." Kristen gave a subtle nod to a woman sitting at the bar.

Megan looked over and then immediately lowered her eyes. "She is not! She's watching the game on the TV behind us."

Stacey waved the woman over. Megan shot her a death glance and looked over at Kristen for support. Kristen refused to meet her eyes. "What are you doing?" Megan shout-whispered.

"Tricia, hey!" Kristen said, standing and embracing the woman. "How have you been?"

"Who is this?" Megan whispered to Stacey through gritted teeth.

"Don't be mad. We thought it might be nice for you to hang

out with someone, you know, human and not totally crazy. She's someone Kristen used to work with." Stacey put her hand on top of Megan's. Megan slapped it with her other hand.

"Are you serious? You're setting me up? *Tonight?* That is not what I asked for, Stacey. I wanted to just kick back with my friends. And after what I just told you about Angeline? I could kill you right now." Megan wished she could just get up and leave, but it wasn't in her blood. She knew they were just trying to help, even if it was wildly inappropriate.

"You said you were over Jessica and ready to move on, and that was months ago, and now with everything that's been going on…obviously I am totally rethinking this strategy right now. I'm sorry, really. I didn't think it through." Stacey looked genuinely apologetic, but it didn't lessen Megan's intense irritation.

"Megan, this is Tricia. We worked together at the *Fog Hollow Sun.* Until she became a bigwig and started at the *Times.* Tricia, this is our friend Megan, she's a real estate appraiser here in town. Can I get you something to drink?" Kristen asked. She seemed to notice Megan's grim expression for the first time and adjusted the neck of her sweater.

Tricia nodded. "Another gin and tonic would be great." She took the empty seat next to Megan. She was attractive, with short brown hair and bright blue eyes. "How's the housing market?"

Instead of sulking, which was what Megan really wanted to do, she decided to put on a less-than-miserable face and try to act like the people person she was most decidedly *not*. She cleared her throat and took a sip of her margarita. "Falling right now, but you know, it's cyclical. With rates rising, it's a purchase market. If you're thinking of selling, now is the time to do it." Megan watched Tricia's reaction to see if she was genuinely interested or just making conversation.

"I see. So, do you want to play pool? Dance?"

Awkward. Megan saw Kristen close her eyes and down half her drink. At least she was coming around to the fact that the setup was a horrible idea. *What the hell. My night out with friends couldn't get any worse. Could it?* "Sure, let's play pool." Megan swallowed a giant mouthful of margarita and slammed her glass on the table. She raised her eyebrows at Stacey in a silent demand for another. Stacey went to the bar immediately.

Tricia put four quarters in the slot and racked the balls. Megan selected a medium-sized pool cue and chalked the top until her fingers were bright blue. She wasn't very good at pool and she really didn't care.

"So, Kristen told me that you're single?" Tricia asked, apparently not well versed in the art of subtlety.

"I am." Megan shot a quick glance around the bar to see if Angeline would magically appear to rescue her from the fresh hell she'd found herself in. Oddly, she was sort of hoping that she would.

"Nice, me too. My last relationship was rough. She was a straight girl who thought she'd give being with a woman a shot. You know, the whole guys suck thing, so maybe a woman is the way to go. I shouldn't have fallen for it, but I did, and big surprise, she's with some dude now. How about you? Have you been single long?" Tricia concentrated as she sank the three ball into the corner pocket.

Megan sighed. She supposed she might as well just lay it all out there. Not exactly first date conversation, but since nothing else about the night was first-date-like, nor did she want it to be first-date-like, she might as well follow the leader. "About six months or so. It wasn't any kind of dramatic breakup, we just sort of grew apart. We still talk once in a while. Man, these drinks are strong," Megan said, polishing off her second.

"Another?" Tricia asked.

"Yup."

Megan scratched on her shot and leaned against the pool table. She was on the right side of buzzed, heading toward drunk at an alarming rate. Since she only drank hard liquor once or twice a year at most, her tolerance was at ground level.

After two more drinks and a good amount of polite

conversation, Kristen and Stacey announced that they were leaving. Stacey wrapped her arms around Megan, bringing her close.

"I'm sorry," she whispered. "We thought it was a good idea."

Megan snorted, her head heavy from the alcohol. "It's fine," she said, a hair louder than she meant to. "She's nice."

"You know you can't drive home, right? Do you want us to take you?" Kristen asked Megan, while saying her good-byes to Tricia.

"No, no I'm good. I'll get a Luber. Or a Ryft."

Kristen and Stacey exchanged skeptical looks, but Tricia stepped in. "I can give her a ride home. We'll just finish up our game and then hit the road. I've been drinking ginger ale since my last G&T when you first got here."

Megan overheard the conversation and decided that it didn't really matter either way, as long as she was delivered to her bedroom in one piece. "Whatever. She can take me home. But she doesn't know where I live!"

Megan watched as the other three chuckled and realized she was probably a little more intoxicated than she had realized.

"Don't worry, I have GPS. Kristen, thank you. I'll give you a call soon," Tricia said, smiling broadly. She must have thought the date was going well. Maybe it was. Megan wasn't sure of anything at that moment.

"You sure?" Stacey asked, looking pointedly at Megan.

"Yeah. I'm sure. Go."

Stacey frowned but took Kristen's hand and headed toward the door. Kristen waved over her shoulder and made the phone gesture with her fingers. Megan nodded, or at least thought she did.

After Tricia sank the eight ball for the third or fourth time, she suggested that they get going. Megan was totally on board with that plan. She was pretty sure she was going to nod off standing up if she didn't get to bed soon.

The cold air hit Megan in the face like a ton of bricks,

sobering her up just a little. She followed Tricia warily to her car. Tricia chirped her locks open with her key fob and opened the passenger side door of a small silver coupe. Megan crouched in, wondering what in the hell she was doing, exactly.

Tricia slid into the driver seat and started the engine. She turned the heat up and rubbed her hands together. "Before I take you home, I just want to thank you for a really nice time. I had fun."

"You're welcome." Megan knew that wasn't the correct response, but she wasn't in the mood to sort out what was.

Before she knew what was happening, Tricia leaned over and kissed her, her lips wet and mushy. Megan felt Tricia's tongue breach her lips, and she put a hand on Tricia's chest. "I'm sorry, I don't want to do this right now."

"Oh, sorry. I got the feeling you were really into me, so I just assumed you wanted me to kiss you."

Megan had no idea how to respond to that. Even in her altered state, she was fairly certain she hadn't made any comments or gestures that would lead Tricia to believe that she'd been "really into her." She seemed nice enough, but that was about it.

"Sorry." The apologies were flying left and right.

"Does that mean you're *not* really into me?" Tricia asked, still facing Megan.

Stacey is dead to me. Megan swallowed. She really should have left with Stacey and Kristen. She'd already be at home, sound asleep with Merlin kneading her calf. "I just don't think… you know, I might throw up, so maybe now isn't the best time for this conversation."

Tricia backed away toward her window. "Okay, no offense, but you can't throw up in my car. Maybe you should go sleep it off in yours or something."

Megan had underestimated. The night clearly *could* get worse. She thought of telling Tricia that she'd be fine until she made it home, but the thought of begging her for a ride made Megan feel even sicker. "Fine. I'll go call for a ride. Thanks."

Megan fumbled with the door handle. She stood up and straightened out her sweater.

"Maybe I'll see you around," Tricia said through the cracked passenger window, before she sped off into the darkness. She even peeled out a little, like a rich villain from an eighties movie.

Megan watched her drive away, dumbfounded. Not that she expected anything from someone she had just met that night, and had summarily rejected, but human decency seemed to dictate that Tricia should have made sure Megan at least made it to her car okay.

Squinting, Megan saw a glint of red on the other side of the parking lot. She made her way there, slowly and with few stumbles. She was proud of herself for staying upright. She wanted to get out of the cold and collect her bearings before calling a ride service. *I am never drinking again.* She reached into her purse for her keys but came up with nothing. She patted down her pockets and looked on the ground around her.

"Fuck. You really didn't learn your fucking lesson about leaving your keys lying around?" she asked herself angrily. Tears welled in her eyes and she started to cry.

Brakes squelched behind Megan, startling her. She jumped and turned around.

"Second time in one day, huh? I take it you need a ride?"

Angeline's window was all the way down, her grinning face a beacon of light. Megan huffed in relief. Relief tinged with shame.

"I don't even know what to say to you right now. I am so embarrassed. I'm drunk and stranded and I lost my keys," Megan said, leaning on Angeline's car.

"Okay. Hop in. I'll park and then I'll run inside to see if you left them in there. Don't cry, we'll find them."

But Megan couldn't help it. She stifled a sob that was mixed with sadness and gratitude and humiliation and exhilaration. She realized, at that moment, there was no one on earth she would rather have had pull up than Angeline.

Megan walked around the front of the car and then flung herself onto the plush leather seat. "Thank you," she whispered.

Angeline covered her hand with her own. Every time they touched, Megan felt like literal sparks were flying out of her skin. "You don't have to thank me. But I hope you don't do this often."

Megan let out a strangled laugh. "I haven't been this drunk since Janet sang at the Super Bowl. Trust me, this is an aberration."

Angeline parked in front of the club and jumped out. She locked the doors behind her and disappeared inside. Megan watched her go, and even drunk she couldn't help but wonder what the feelings that swirled within her stomach were about. Some of it was nausea, sure, but there was something else there. She was developing a…fondness? Or something like that toward Angeline. There was tingle inside her when she saw Angeline exit the club with Megan's keys dangling from her index finger.

"You really do have a problem hanging on to these, don't you?" Angeline said, handing them over. She started the engine and pulled out onto the deserted road.

"Apparently. This really is embarrassing. I'm so sorry that I summoned you or whatever I did that brought you here." Megan chewed on her lip.

"I had a feeling your date wasn't going to end well. When I first drove by, I saw you in the car with that woman, and thought maybe I misread something. But then a few minutes later your discomfort was unmistakable," Angeline said, not taking her eyes off the road.

"Oh, it wasn't a date. It wasn't like that. My friends thought I needed a distraction from everything, and they decided I should—I don't even know—hook up? Trust me, I am super pissed at them for this."

Angeline smiled. "You don't need to explain yourself to me, you know."

That was true. So why did Megan feel the need to make sure Angeline knew that the setup, or whatever it was, wasn't her idea? She could analyze that later, but for the moment, she just wanted to make that point clear. "I know. But I really wasn't into it."

They pulled up in front of Megan's house. Megan just sat for a second, deciding how she was going to make it to the door when the world was spinning diagonally. Luckily, she didn't need to. Angeline opened her door and took her by the arm, walking her steadily up toward her front door.

"Do you need me to walk you in?" Angeline asked.

"No, I'm okay. Wait. Yes."

Angeline took the key from Megan's hand and unlocked the door. She walked her into the bedroom, where Megan sat on the edge of her bed. Merlin was sprawled out on his bed and didn't even bother to look up when they came into the room.

"Here," Angeline said, handing Megan a pair of sweatpants hanging on the edge of her treadmill. She grabbed a T-shirt from the top of Megan's dresser. "I don't know if these are clean or not, but I don't think it matters much. I'm pretty sure you're going to want to take a shower the second you wake up."

Megan nodded. She pulled on the hem of her sweater, but suddenly all of her strength was completely gone. "Can you help?" Mortification no longer registered on Megan's radar. She just wanted to be comfy.

"Uh, yeah, sure." Angeline rubbed her hands together to warm them and pulled Megan's sweater over her head. She quickly threw the T-shirt on over her. Megan lay back on the bed and unzipped her jeans. Angeline pulled them off from the ankles and shimmied the sweats up Megan's legs. She circled her under her arms and lifted Megan off the bed. Megan rested her head on Angeline's shoulder.

"Why are you being so nice to me?"

Angeline cleared her throat. "I don't know, maybe I'm just nice. I like you."

"I don't know why. I'm a hot mess."

"A little, yeah." Angeline laughed. "But who isn't?"

"I like you too, Angeline. Tell me about the thirties," Megan said. She sat up on her bed and threw the blanket over her feet.

"The thirties?"

"Yeah. I need to concentrate on something that isn't my churning stomach."

Angeline laughed lightly and sat on the edge of Megan's bed. She squeezed her toe. "Okay. Well, I spent most of the thirties in Maryland, I think. Delaware for a little while. Art was huge at the time, and really coming into its own. Movies were also becoming more of a mainstream thing. It was spectacular watching that technology just kind of evolve. I got to meet Clark Gable. His ears really were that big, even in person." She frowned. "You look pretty pale. Why don't you lie down?"

She did feel a little woozy. Megan fell back on her pillow and pulled the covers up to her neck. Angeline went to the kitchen, got a glass of water, and put it on Megan's nightstand. She brushed a piece of hair that was hanging in Megan's face back behind her ear.

"Did I take you away from the clinic again?" Megan asked, her voice barely a whisper. Her face was smushed into her pillow. She struggled to stay awake, really wanting to talk to Angeline a little bit more.

"No, I had tonight off. You have my number, so if you want to talk about anything that's, you know, not dire, call me. If it is dire, I'm sure I'll know about it."

"Can you stay? What if I get sick? I don't want be alone and choke on my own vomit."

"Ew. But okay. I guess I can stay. Where do you keep your blankets?"

Megan mumbled something, but sleep meant the spinning stopped, and she let herself drift away.

Some hours later, Megan stirred. The events of the evening came flooding back to her, and if she weren't already lying down, she would have hung her head in shame. Angeline must have left once she realized Megan was sleeping. Megan lifted her brick of a head and looked around her room. There, in front of the door, on Megan's recliner that she must have dragged into the room, slept Angeline. Merlin slept in a ball at her feet. Megan's heart filled with appreciation. She wanted to get out of bed and go to her, hug her, thank her for everything. But her earlier nausea had been replaced with a pounder of a headache. Megan laid her head back down against her pillow and smiled, drifting off into sleep once again.

CHAPTER TEN

Charleston, South Carolina, 1948

The seven-inch TV screen held Angeline rapt. Irving Berlin was on the *Toast of the Town* with Ed Sullivan. Even though the sound was a bit muffled, his version of "God Bless America" brought tears to her eyes. She wiped them away with a laugh. Her cold exterior was such a lie.

She leaned forward in the wingback chair when she heard a noise from the kitchen. The old sugar plantation that Kathryn had converted into a home for the two of them was big and airy and overwhelming. Most of the décor belonged to Kathryn, from the Steinway piano that no one ever played, to her prized katana blade that she'd brought back from Japan, to the hand-painted watercolor of a maple tree in autumn. Angeline had preferred the small cabin they'd been living in deep inside Hitchcock Woods, but Kathryn wanted something more glamorous. She didn't seem to notice that the old house they were living in was more than a little run-down, and the willows surrounding it were tilting forward more and more every day.

They'd been together for more than twenty years. Angeline had vague memories of her past life, but for the most part they'd faded into sepia-tinged images that occasionally crossed her mind. She remembered playing outside with her sister. Stella's favorite game was marbles, but she always cheated. Somehow Angeline always went back in the house with fewer marbles than she'd gone outside with, and Stella's pouch was just a little bit fuller. Even though Stella was just a year younger, Angeline's parents acted like she was the baby of the family, so it wasn't worth the fight.

She remembered her father, gentle and easygoing. He used to call her his angel. Angeline would help her father outside in the garden while Stella did housework with her mother. It was their special time to talk about the world. Angeline cherished those memories with her father because she remembered feeling like a grown-up, like her opinion mattered and he was interested in what she had to say. Also, because those were the brightest colored memories she had of him.

She remembered her mother most of all. Her mother wasn't a meek or sweet lady by any means. She was brazen and gruff and complemented Angeline's father perfectly. She had no problem telling her husband when she disagreed with him. While growing up, Angeline thought she was too strict and she liked to meddle a bit too much and expected more of her than anyone else. They argued and fought with each other while her father tried to be the mediator and Stella played the role of perfect daughter. But then when she had turned eighteen, her mother had said, "My daddy always told me that the only way to avoid disappointment was to expect nothing from nobody. You're the only one I've found that that doesn't apply to." Angeline's biggest antagonist had been, in truth, her biggest supporter and her biggest fan. Her mother had known that the sky was the limit for her elder child, so she tried to boost her up as high as she was able to. It might have included some shoves and kicks along the way, but her aim was always true. And it was her mother that Angeline missed the most.

Benjamin was little more than a phantom in the recesses of Angeline's mind. She knew that she'd been married and that she'd been content, but even Ben's face was just a smudge. He'd probably remarried once they'd given up the search for Angeline, and she hoped that he had. He deserved to have a happy life. She was thankful they'd never had children. Though she didn't know firsthand, she could only imagine that leaving a child behind would have been unbearable.

It was in those moments of nostalgia that Angeline resented Kathryn the most.

"Who's there?" Angeline asked, switching off the television. Ed Sullivan would have to wait.

"Sorry, miss. I didn't mean to alarm you."

"That's all right, George. What can I do for you?" Angeline asked. Kathryn had insisted that they employ a couple of hired hands to keep the plantation in good working order. Angeline didn't have the heart to tell either of the men that they weren't very good at it.

"You have a letter. From up north." George handed her a battered envelope, dirty from handling and crumpled from the passage of time.

"Thank you, George," Angeline said, distracted. The return address was Lowell, Massachusetts. "That'll be all, but if you could tend to the well, I would appreciate it. The water has an unpleasant smell."

"Of course, miss." George nodded, and watched her for another moment, his expression inscrutable, before he headed back outside.

Angeline sat with the letter on her lap before opening it. She'd only given her address to one person, a private investigator who took his money and never asked questions. He was to contact her if anything of note happened within the Vallencourt family. No one was to know anything about it. All correspondence was handled through the post, and to date, there had only been one letter, some years back. It had announced the death of her father, given the PI's condolences, and included a request for a certified check.

Angeline turned the letter over in her hands, fearing its contents. She hoped that it was happy news, but she couldn't imagine what that happy news would entail. The hollow in her stomach told her that it was something she didn't necessarily want to know.

She slit the top of the envelope open with her fingernail. Inside was a single sheet of paper, folded into thirds. She sighed and unfolded the letter.

Dear Mrs. Miles,

It has come to my attention that Lucille Vallencourt, your mother, is in failing health at Lowell General Hospital. Her case of influenza has turned into a terminal lung infection, and the doctors do not believe she will recover. My sources tell me that she is unlikely to last the week.

With sincere condolences,

Albert. F. McMahon, PI

Please send along a cashier's check for the previously agreed upon amount.

Angeline refolded the letter and placed it back inside the envelope. The lump in her throat threatened to choke her, but she decided that she had to be rational. She knew the day would come. She knew that her family wouldn't live forever. Even though she hadn't seen them in over twenty years, the bond was still tighter than she'd realized.

She'd be forty-eight years old if Kathryn hadn't turned her. Angeline looked down at her hand and wiggled her fingers. Still the hand of a young woman. She'd missed so much. This life, the freedom afforded her, was supposed to be better. Not having to abide by the human world's imposed rules, not having to succumb to the natural order of old age and death. If she were being honest, wilting away in the confines of isolation didn't seem all that preferable to the perils of aging naturally.

She wondered if it would have been easier to receive the news after her mother had already passed away. It would have been over with, with nothing for her to do but mourn, like she had done for her father. But knowing her mother was lying on her deathbed nearly a thousand miles away presented its own challenge. Angeline closed her eyes and rested her head on the back of the chair.

Suddenly, she stood up and ran to her bedroom. She didn't care what Kathryn would say about it. Angeline was going to say good-bye to her mother, and neither Kathryn nor any other force on earth was going to stop her.

She threw some clothes into a bag and grabbed a pile of cash from her nightstand drawer. Kathryn's constant theft was exhausting but useful.

"Going somewhere?" Kathryn asked, appearing in Angeline's door frame. She was filing her nails with an emery board.

"Yes," Angeline answered, not looking up. "I'm going back to Massachusetts for a while. I have some business I need to attend to."

Kathryn raised her eyebrows in mock surprise. "You've been dead for twenty-two years. What business could you possibly have in Massachusetts?"

Anger was building inside her, but Angeline knew she needed to keep her cool. "It's nothing, Kathryn. Please just allow me to do this."

"Who's dying? Mother? Sister? The widower?"

"I didn't say anyone was dying." *Damn her.* Kathryn could always read her like an open book.

"The only 'business' that would send you back to Massachusetts is death. But those people are no longer your family, Angeline. I've tried to tell you that time and time again. To them, you're a distant memory. When they think of you now, maybe they get a small pang of sadness, or maybe a fleeting smile of remembrance. But they couldn't recall your voice, or your mannerisms, or even the details of your face if they tried. Let sleeping dogs lie. There is no reason to reopen healed wounds."

Maybe those wounds had healed for Kathryn, but for Angeline, they were still raw and open. Sure, she enjoyed herself when they traveled, and when she wasn't consumed with debilitating boredom from being cooped up in the house or walking through deserted streets alone, she usually felt okay. But the loneliness she felt was deep, and it was real. Kathryn was a companion, but Angeline didn't love her or think of her as family. Most of the time she didn't even really like her. She resented her and begrudged what she had done to her. But the thought of being utterly alone was terrifying. So she tolerated her.

"It's my mother. She's very sick, and I'm going to see her. She'll think I'm the angel of death, or the welcoming committee into heaven, and then she'll be able to go peacefully. I'm not staying long. Just long enough to tell her that I love her and that I've never forgotten her." Angeline pulled a heavy coat out of her armoire. She had no need for it in South Carolina, but Massachusetts wasn't as forgiving, even in early spring.

Kathryn folded her arms over her chest. "No."

Angeline swallowed. "I didn't ask permission, Kathryn. I'm going to see her. I'll be back in just a few days. There is a flight service to Boston out of Lexington County, so I'll take that to shorten the time I'll be away."

"And if you should get stranded in a field somewhere, waiting for help in the midday sun?"

"That's very unlikely to happen. Airplane travel is very safe, even the television ads say so. And if it does, then I guess I'll burn up while the rest of the passengers watch in horror. Maybe they'll think I had a high fever."

"Kid all you want, Angeline, but I can't allow you to reveal our existence just so you can make yourself feel better with a kiss and a deathbed confession," Kathryn said. She stared into Angeline's defiant eyes.

"You would really deny me this? A simple good-bye to ease a lifetime of heartache and regret?" Tears blurred her vision, but Angeline didn't let them fall. She wouldn't let Kathryn see her vulnerable. She didn't have the heart to see that she was hurting Angeline; she would only use it to her advantage if she did.

"Have I not been good to you, all these years? I've provided for you, and protected you, and tried to make sure you were happy. Why do you always make it sound like I've deprived you of a better life?"

To Angeline's surprise, Kathryn appeared crestfallen. Did she really think this was better than a normal, human life? To subsist on blood and to be eternally denied sunlight and to skulk around like a common criminal in fear of persecution and death?

"Kathryn, you know that I wouldn't have chosen this for myself if I had been given a choice. That isn't a secret. I also didn't think it was a secret that while you do seem to have my safety as a priority, you're controlling and condescending and righteous," Angeline said. She had alluded to all of those things over the years, but that was the first time she had said them point-blank. She wasn't sure if she should brace for Kathryn's reaction.

But there was no explosion of fury or sadness. Kathryn nodded slowly. "I suppose I've always known that I wasn't the soul mate you'd envisioned for yourself. Time has marched on, and you've stayed with me. We've both had our share of lovers and relationships over the years, but we always ended up together."

Because I'm afraid of you. Angeline knew that had always been a driving force for their seemingly inseparable union. *And because I'm afraid of an existence without you.*

"Yes, we have," Angeline said. "And I suspect we always will, because, really, what else have we got?"

"Well, if that isn't a rousing endorsement of our friendship, then I don't know what is."

"But, Kathryn, it's the truth. If I go out and make a friend tomorrow, I can only have them in my life for, what? Ten years, tops? And then they'll start to question why I'm not aging. I'd have to make up some illness that keeps me from the sun. If my anger or my hunger ever got the best of me, I'd have a lot of explaining to do about my dental work. It just can't happen. And if for some reason I did tell them what I really am, and they accepted it, they'd be dead after what, forty, fifty years? And I'd have to go through the grieving process all over again. It's not worth it." The more she spoke, the more suffocated Angeline felt by the life she'd been given.

"You've proved my point about why you can't go back to Massachusetts. Someone could recognize you. Your mother could have a panic attack at the sight of you and have you arrested. *It's not worth it*," Kathryn said, mockingly.

"I'm going," Angeline said through gritted teeth. She brushed by Kathryn, her shoulder bumping Kathryn's into the doorway.

Angeline knew that Kathryn could have stopped her if she'd really wanted to. She was stronger than her, faster than her, and much more adept at slinking in and out of places unnoticed. All she would have had to do was physically restrain Angeline and that would have kept her in place.

Yet she didn't. Angeline kept waiting for Kathryn to barricade the door, then to rip the engine out of her car, then to appear on the road to the airport so that Angeline would swerve into a tree. But she did none of those things.

Angeline made it to the ticket counter of the airport in just over two hours from the time she left Charleston. The flight to Boston was leaving in three hours and cost nearly half of the cash Angeline had brought with her. Flying was a rich man's luxury.

A woman of about thirty-five, short and dressed in a tweed swing dress, entered the restroom. Angeline dropped her bags on the nearest bench and followed her in.

"Shh," she commanded, pushing the woman up against the wall. She covered her mouth with her hand, the woman's terrified eyes wide and unblinking. Angeline thrust her into a stall and slid the lock across. Angeline met the woman's eyes with her own, compelling her to relax. The hypnotization only caused momentary stasis, so Angeline had to work fast. She positioned her mouth beneath the woman's ear, so there wouldn't be any obvious wound, and she punctured the skin easily. Angeline drank until she was sated, the euphoria as strong as it was twenty years ago. The high from the first rush of blood was unlike anything Angeline had experienced in her human life. It was intoxicating.

"Sorry," she whispered, more out of habit than anything else. The woman was passed out, but she would come to soon enough, wondering what the hell had happened to her. Angeline positioned her on the closed toilet seat so that she wouldn't fall over. She opened the stall door quietly, saw there was no one else in the restroom, washed her hands, and went to the waiting room to wait for her boarding call.

CHAPTER ELEVEN

Fog Hollow, Massachusetts, current day

Megan sat at her desk, adding the finishing remarks to the appraisal she needed to send over. She was glad to be back at work, sort of, but it made what had happened at the gas station, and for that matter, Angeline, take on a dreamlike quality. There were times when Megan had to remind herself that those events really had taken place. Two people were dead, and if not for Angeline, she would have certainly made it three.

She was still angry at Stacey and Kristen for blindsiding her at the club, but she knew she needed to cave sooner or later. They'd sent her a hundred apology texts, asking her to call or stop by or *something.* She'd mostly ignored them except for an "*it's fine*" and a quick recap of how the night had ended, which only encouraged them to send a new flurry of sorrys. Kristen promised to never speak to Tricia again, which Megan knew might have been a tad extreme, but still made her kind of happy.

She hadn't seen or heard from Angeline since that Friday morning when she'd woken to find her recliner back in the living room and a bottle of aspirin on her bedside table. It had been more than a week since then, and Megan had been trying to figure out a way contact her casually. She'd typed and deleted text after text, not knowing what to say to her. *Thank you* sounded too clinical. *Come over tonight* sounded too pathetic, like she wanted to repay

Angeline for helping her home. *I'd like to see you again* sounded too date-ish. But in reality, Megan didn't hate that idea. She was pretty comfortable with the notion that Angeline wasn't going to hurt her. She still had lots of questions but didn't want to seem too pushy. Although that ship could very possibly have already sailed. What was the protocol for going on a date with a vampire? Did Angeline do that sort of thing? Was she even attracted to Megan? Megan felt like she was fifteen, only this time instead of a flip phone, she was turning her iPhone over and over, wondering if she should make the first move.

Oh, the hell with it. She punched Angeline's number into the message box and sent a quick text.

Hey, it's Megan. Do you want to come over later? Maybe get some pizza or something?

Megan bit her lip while she stared at the screen, willing Angeline to respond. She decided to distract herself with organizing her silverware drawer. Three forks in and she was ready to call it quits, but then her cell phone dinged. She nearly scared Merlin to death by the way she leapt over the chaise toward the coffee table.

Sure. I have to work at 8, so would 6 be ok? I'll grab pizza on my way over.

Megan checked the time. It was nearly five, so that didn't give her much time to prepare.

Yes, that's perfect. See you then!

Angeline responded with a thumbs-up emoji and a smiley face.

Megan's stomach fluttered. For a brief moment, she wondered if Angeline was doing some kind of supernatural hoodoo on her. But really, what would be the point? Angeline had had plenty of opportunity to make a move on Megan, but she'd always remained distant and respectful. Megan couldn't come up with a reason that made sense if Angeline had wanted anything more from her.

She wasn't looking for a relationship. Or at least, not in

any kind of active way. Relationships in general didn't usually end well and were rarely worth the effort and heartache. At least in Megan's estimation. She had ended things with Jessica six months ago and had been pretty content on her own. She'd been with Jessica for just over two years, but they'd maintained separate lives. They hadn't moved in together or shared a bank account. Jessica had only met Aunt Susie once, and hadn't stayed for more than a few minutes once she realized that Megan wasn't alone. They both enjoyed their freedom, so the nature of their relationship had worked. But when it became harder and harder to get in touch with her, and Jessica would go an entire week without calling, she'd decided that maybe it wasn't working anymore. When she suggested that maybe they should take a break, Jessica had readily agreed.

Two days later, Kristen saw Jessica at Pantsuit slow dancing with another woman. And then kissing her. Megan had wanted to rush over to her house and scream in her face, throw herself on her knees and yell "why" at the heavens, but decided that she obviously hadn't meant that much to Jessica in the first place, so there was no reason to make a fool of herself for something she hadn't been about to fight for anyway. Her ego was bruised, but it healed pretty fast.

Megan realized that she did miss certain things about being with someone. Nighttime snuggles. A TV watching partner. Someone to fight with about where they would go out to dinner. Good sex. But could Angeline really be that person? Someone who craved human blood and was never going to look a day over twenty-five no matter how long they stayed together? After all, Megan was going to get old. She'd *look* old. Angeline had money, she'd traveled, she'd presumably been with…a lot of people over the last nine decades. Megan could count her intimate partners on one hand. And she didn't even need to use all of the fingers. How could she live up to the expectations that Angeline undoubtedly had?

A knock at the door interrupted Megan's brooding. She

stood, straightened her shirt, and ran her hand through her hair. She opened the door to find Angeline standing there with a pizza box in her hand.

"Thank you," Megan said, taking the box from her hands. She laid it on the kitchen table while Angeline removed her jacket. "I'm sorry, I didn't even think to ask. Do you even, you know, eat pizza?"

Angeline smiled. "I do. I enjoy the taste very much. It has no nutritional value, of course, but I don't think that's why most people eat it anyway. Thank you for the invitation," she said, leaning in to hug Megan.

Megan hugged her tightly, inhaling her fresh scent. She was captivating. She lamented the loss of contact when Angeline pulled away. "No, thank you for coming. And good point," Megan said, pouring soda into two glasses. She noticed Angeline was already wearing her scrubs. "Have you worked at the clinic long?"

"About a year. I found this town on my way to the Berkshires and fell in love. So I found an apartment, a job, and settled down for a while. It doesn't pay very much, but I'm not doing it for the money."

"Does anyone else know?"

Angeline shook her head. She took a sip of her soda. "No. Like I told you before, it's no easy feat to tell a person. It either ends in disbelief or them trying to kill me, although it's a hell of a lot easier in this decade. Less superstition and more personal privacy, overall. It's really just easier to keep it under wraps."

Megan watched as Angeline took a delicate bite of her pizza. Her long brown hair was down around her shoulders, and that smirk that she seemed to wear so often was playing at her lips. Her full, pink, inviting lips.

"It's good."

Megan cleared her throat. She hoped Angeline hadn't noticed her staring at her. "It is. Thank you again. I know I asked a million questions that night in your office. But can I ask you just a few more?"

"I expected nothing less."

"I'm sorry, I just feel like I need to get these out of the way so that I can get to know the…other parts of you. Are you sure you don't mind?" Megan asked.

"Really, it's fine. What's on your mind?"

"Do you have any vampire friends?"

"Not anymore."

"Have you had any relationships?" Megan asked, looking away. It felt like a strangely intrusive question.

"Well, in my old life I was married. If you can believe it. Because most of the time, I can't. Feels like twelve lifetimes ago, not just one. But I assume you mean since I was turned. I have had a few relationships, yes. One serious. She and I were together for a long time. The others were fleeting."

Interesting revelations. So Angeline *was* interested in women. A quick beat of excitement pulsed through her. Though Megan wondered why, over the course of ninety years, Angeline would have only one lasting relationship? With the popularity of vampires (fake ones, but still), and the way she looked, it wasn't like Angeline would have had any trouble finding willing participants.

"What happened?" Megan asked. She wasn't sure if that was crossing the line or not, but since Angeline seemed to be open to sharing, she might as well ask.

"She died."

Angeline didn't seem to want to elaborate, so Megan wasn't going to push. She leaned forward. "Do you have any special powers?"

"I can't fly or anything like that. I can jump pretty high though, like a cat. My hearing is sharp, my eyesight is amazingly clear, I'm faster and stronger than most people, and I can heal from just about anything."

"And you really think this just some kind of blood mutation? Not supernatural?" Megan asked.

Angeline sat back in her chair and sighed. "I don't know. Certain things point to the supernatural. Immortality is a big one, obviously. I've never seen the face of God, or the Devil for that matter. It's not like those TV shows where there's a vampire, and then there are werewolves, ghosts, mermaids, zombies, and whatever. I've never encountered any other non-human beings except for vampires. And it's not like the world is flooded with them either. You have to seek them out."

"So there aren't any vampire hierarchies or covens or anything like that? You don't have a governor to answer to?" The media had a lot to answer for. They'd gotten so much wrong.

"Not at all. I answer to no one and I prefer to keep it that way."

"How did you become a vampire?"

"Just how you would imagine. I was bit by a vampire, and then forced to drink her blood. If you have enough in you when your body dies, you'll turn. I was turned by a woman named Kathryn. Not the most benevolent of creatures. She's not around anymore, which is a very good thing."

Megan watched Angeline's face grow darker. She decided it might be a good idea to lighten the mood. "Do you do normal things, like watch TV, read books, play games?"

It seemed to work. Angeline smiled broadly. "Absolutely. I've seen just about every sitcom you can imagine, and I was a big fan of *Dark Shadows*. It's funny how many things people get wrong about vampires. I like to read self-help books and biographies, mostly. But I'll read just about anything. E-readers might just be my favorite invention of this century. I don't play a lot of games, because I don't really have many people to play them with. I would, though. If you want to break out Trivial Pursuit or something, I'm all for it."

Megan considered her for a second. "Does it get lonely?"

"Does what get lonely?"

"Being so isolated all the time."

"Honestly?" Angeline asked, rubbing the back of her neck. "Yes. It does. But if I want to maintain my anonymity, and not fear for my safety every day, I don't have much of a choice. Here, let me help you clean up."

The abrupt tone shift made it sound like Angeline was done with the Q&A portion of the evening. Megan supposed she couldn't blame her. She probably wanted to talk about her favorite places to travel and the cute dogs she doted on at the clinic, and all Megan wanted to talk about were religious relics and retractable fangs.

Angeline stood at the sink washing out her cup. Her hair fell in perfect waves down the length of her back. Megan's heart began to beat faster, and she wondered if Angeline was able to pick up on the subtle differences in her emotions. That blood bond thing they shared was ambiguous at best. *This is it. If I don't make a move now, I never will.* The doubts she'd had earlier were beginning to creep back in, but she brushed them aside. She had plenty to offer. Megan sucked in a breath and readied herself. She walked softly up to her and put her hand on Angeline's back. Angeline stiffened, but didn't make any move to stop her. Megan slid her arms around Angeline's waist, and brought her lips to the exposed skin of Angeline's neck. Angeline sighed into it and turned her head, allowing Megan easier access.

The electricity of Angeline's skin against Megan's mouth confirmed it. This was *definitely* what Megan wanted. Any thoughts of Angeline's true nature or what that would mean for them danced right out of her head at the feeling of Angeline's body melting into hers.

Angeline turned fully, so that their bodies were pressed against each other. She leaned forward, bringing their lips softly together. Megan moaned involuntarily, but her desire for Angeline pushed any embarrassment she might have felt deep into the recesses of her emotions.

Megan sought to deepen the kiss, parting her lips and sliding her tongue along the fullness of Angeline's lips. It was Angeline's turn to moan, and when she did, she pulled slightly away. She took Megan's hands into her own and looked into her eyes.

"Megan," she said, her voice deep and thick. "I can't do this. I'm so sorry."

Megan was taken aback. She took a step backward, inserting about a foot of space between them. "Was it something I did?"

"No, not at all. I want this too. I want you. Believe me, I do," Angeline said. "But it just isn't possible. I speak from experience. Our two worlds could never intertwine the way we would want them to."

For a moment, Megan considered the idea of meaningless sex. She was insanely turned on, and the thought of Angeline walking out the door made her weak-kneed. But she knew that it was probably a very bad idea. Megan was attracted to Angeline, certainly, but she suspected there was more to it than that. Sex would only make it worse.

"It would obviously be a challenge, but I don't see why we couldn't at least try. Maybe we'll decide we don't even like each other after a few dates," Megan said. She was trying to lighten the mood, but her heart felt like it was weighted down by a boulder. She'd known Angeline for less than a month. There was no reason on earth she should feel this emotionally invested, but she couldn't help it.

"I highly doubt that," Angeline said softly. She ran the back of her fingertips down Megan's cheek.

Her touch felt like heaven. Megan tried to stop the words from spilling out, but her lips betrayed her. "I just think you're being a little too fatalistic. Haven't you ever seen *Twilight*? They made it work!" Ugh. Bordering on pathetic, at least in her own mind, but Megan feared that if Angeline walked out that door that it would be the last time she'd ever see her.

Angeline's eyes glimmered with a coating of tears. "That's not real life, Megan. It's a glamorized version of a tragic existence. What it's really about is loneliness and death and building a fortress around yourself. It's not all bad, obviously, or there would be no reason to go on. But for the most part, it's nothing more than a curse. A terminal illness, but instead of death, we continue to live while we watch everyone around us grow old and die. One day you realize that the only way to stop the heartbreak is to stop opening yourself up to it. I'm sorry, Megan. I can't go through it again."

Angeline grasped Megan's face, one hand on each side, and their lips crashed together in a fury of heat and sorrow. Megan was speechless as Angeline pulled away and walked out, closing the door tightly behind her.

Megan stood in her kitchen as the quiet threatened to overtake her. Why did Angeline stay once Megan had woken up on that cold grass in the parking lot? She could have just saved her and taken off, and Megan could have just assumed some Good Samaritan had rescued her. But no. Angeline stayed and then showed up over and over again and smiled at Megan with that cocky smirk and made her want her like she'd never wanted anyone, or anything, before. She was thirty-two years old, for God's sake. Stable. Comfortable. Content. And Angeline swept in and turned everything on its head. Megan sat at the table and cried into her hands. Angeline's Mustang rumbled down the street, growing more and more distant, leaving nothing in its wake but the steady hum of the refrigerator and Megan's confusion.

Chapter Twelve

Lowell, Massachusetts, 1948

The hospital hallways were dim, the lights low so they didn't disturb the sleeping patients. Angeline walked nervously through the double doors to the cardiac wing, compulsively checking for the room number the receptionist had written down for her. The hallways twisted and turned like a disinfectant-tinged maze. She finally found door number 1032, which was slightly ajar. She pushed softly, the nurses at their main station paying her no attention.

The room was dark except for a small nightlight near the window. Angeline pushed back the curtain separating the beds, though the one nearer the door was empty, thankfully. She gasped at the sight before her.

Though the clipboard hanging from the foot of the rollaway bed read Millicent Vallencourt, Angeline would have scoffed if someone had pointed out this woman as her mother. Gone was the robust woman with the dark brown hair and judgmental blue eyes and a smile that betrayed her stern demeanor. In her place was a frail shadow, her once-thick hair thin and white, her skin sallow and papery. On her ring finger, the thin gold band with the small diamond in the center skewed to the left, her delicate finger no longer able to support its weight. Angeline remembered that wedding ring well. Her mother wore it no matter what. Gardening, washing dishes, scrubbing the bathtub. "The only person who's going to take this ring off my finger is an undertaker," she'd say.

"Who's there?" the reedy voice asked from the confines of the hospital bed. That voice. Though it was quiet and hoarse, there was no mistaking it.

Angeline dropped to her knees, all muscle abandoning her. She stifled a sob as best she could, but tears poured from her eyes. "It's me, Mom. I'm here. It's me, and I am so, so sorry."

Her mother stirred, opening both of her eyes. She tried to sit up but couldn't. "No, it can't be. It can't be."

Angeline reached up and clasped her mother's hand. She brought her face closer, willing herself to stop crying. "It's me."

"Angeline. My Angeline. Why have you stayed away for so long? I knew it. I knew you'd come back someday. Everyone thought that you were dead, but I never accepted it. I never felt that part of myself disappear completely. Oh, my Angeline," she repeated, cupping Angeline's face in her arthritic hand. "My eyes are playing tricks on me. You haven't aged a bit."

"I didn't want to stay away, I promise you. I just…I couldn't come back. Something happened, and I had to leave. I would have come back if I could have," Angeline said, the words spilling out. She had never been as angry at herself as she was at that moment. Why the *fuck* had she let Kathryn control her for so long? Why didn't she tell her to piss off, and come back to Massachusetts? Was she really so afraid of death at Kathryn's hand? Her mother would never have outed her to anyone. Deep down, she'd always known that. She gave up her one constant for an unsteady allegiance with someone she could barely tolerate.

"I've missed you. I feel like I could just burst. It's never been the same since the day you went missing. If you're in some kind of trouble—"

"No, Mom. I'm okay. I wasn't, but now I am. I'm sorry it took me so long to realize what I've done," Angeline said. Her heart, which she was so sure she had sufficiently walled up over the years, was shattering into minuscule pieces.

"Stop apologizing," her mother said, grimacing in pain. "You're here now. That's what matters. I just wish I could be sure that you're real."

"I'm really here. Where's Stella? Does she have any children? Why are you alone?" Angeline asked, although she quickly regretted it. No need to point out the fact that the hospital room was quiet and empty.

"Stella was here earlier today. She has one child, a son. He's overseas. Somewhere in the Mediterranean, I think. Paul. He's a good boy. Tell me, Angeline, are you happy?"

"Yes," Angeline lied, tears still rolling down her cheeks. She wondered if her nephew even knew she existed. "Happier now."

"Good," she whispered, patting Angeline's hand. "Good. I wish we had more time. But I want you to know that I never forgot about you, and I never stopped loving you."

"I'm not leaving, Mom. We have time. I'm right here." Angeline clutched on to her fragile hand as hard as she could without hurting her.

"But I'm tired, Angie. I'm so tired. It's been so hard..."

Angeline closed her eyes. She wanted to hoist her mother over her shoulder and rescue her from this desolate and morbid place and bring her outside to watch the sunrise, to watch the dandelions sway to the beat of the wind. To stop at Elliot's for a hot dog and a root beer, if they were even still in business. But reality was a cold and unfeeling beast.

"Rest, Mom. I love you and I wish I could do things differently. Just rest." Angeline stayed on her knees, afraid if she let go of her mother's hand she would spin out of control and fall into an abyss from which should never rise.

The clock on the wall ticked loudly, signaling the eternity that passed with every minute. Angeline felt her mother's pulse grow weaker and weaker, but the dire prognosis on the clipboard told her that even if she called for help, no one was going to do anything. All machines had been turned off, and there were no oxygen tents in sight. Millicent Vallencourt was a dying woman, and no one planned to do a damn thing about it.

"I'm sorry," Angeline whispered. Was it really possible that she had returned just in time for her mother's exit from the world? That was the kind of thing that happened in soap operas. A long-lost child swooping in just in time to say good-bye. Yet here she was. Maybe it was true. Maybe her mother needed permission to let her body shut down. Fitting that Angeline should be the one to grant that wish. "I'm sorry." She repeated it over and over again until her mother's hand fell limply onto the bed. She was gone.

Standing on wobbly legs, Angeline wiped her eyes and took a deep breath. She leaned over and kissed her mother's forehead. Before the sadness could overwhelm her again, Angeline slipped out of the hospital room and down the hallway while the nurses began their overnight rounds.

❖

"I didn't think you'd come back," Kathryn said, her legs draped over the arms of a chair in the living room. She didn't look up when Angeline walked in.

"I didn't think I would either, to be honest. I didn't want to, if I'm being *really* honest." Anger coursed through Angeline's veins. She was angry at Kathryn, angry at herself, and angry at whoever the sonofabitch was who started this whole vampire nonsense. The constant doubt about making it on her own, alone in an unfriendly world with no one who understood her, was getting a bit tedious. Even after all this time, she couldn't imagine living in a world where no one knew who—and what—she really was.

"I'm not surprised. Did you accomplish what you set out to do?"

Angeline clenched her teeth. She could feel her gums twitching. "Yes. I did."

"Did she scream at the sight of her daughter's ghost, or did she embrace her little baby vamp like no time has passed at all?" Kathryn flipped a page in her magazine.

"She died."

Kathryn didn't say she was sorry or offer any condolences, but Angeline was pleased that she knew enough to let it go. Otherwise, Angeline would have ripped her throat out. Tried to, anyway.

"While you were away, I did some soul searching. All those years ago, I decided I needed a friend—a companion—and I was lucky enough to find you," Kathryn said, her voice dripping with sweet sarcasm. "Maybe you need something similar. I'd like you to meet Charlotte."

"Who?"

A woman who appeared to be in her twenties walked out of the kitchen, drying her hands on a towel. "Oh, you must be Angeline. I'm Charlotte."

Angeline raised her eyebrows at Kathryn, whose lips were turned up in amusement. "Charlotte is going to stay with us for a while. She's photosensitive, so she too is unable to go out into the sunlight. She's sensitive to our plight."

"You mean—"

"Yes, Angeline. She knows."

"Oh, don't worry about me. Your secret is safe. I've always been very interested in the paranormal, since I wondered for a while if I was actually one of you. It took the doctors quite some time to diagnose me. I went on a ghost hunting mission with Frederick Bligh once. It was life-altering," Charlotte said, leaning against the arm of the velvet couch.

Trying not to roll her eyes, Angeline cleared her throat. "Did you see any ghosts?"

"No. But there was definitely a presence in that old house.

Their equipment was vibrating and beeping and making all kinds of noises. It was really creepy." Charlotte pushed the blond hair that had fallen out of her barrette away from her face. She reminded Angeline of Carole Lombard in *Nothing Sacred*.

"Well," Angeline said, sighing. "I've had a very long and trying few days, so if you'll both excuse me, I'm going to bed."

She picked her suitcase up and carried it to her bedroom, which was a welcome sight even though she'd wished she could have just stayed in Massachusetts. She'd thought about contacting Stella, but she was pretty sure Stella wouldn't have been as accepting of her return as their mother. There'd be far more questions, things she couldn't answer. Her mother's rheumy eyes might have shown her a young-looking Angeline, but certainly not just how young looking she actually was. Appearing on Stella's doorstep was just too risky. Angeline wasn't sure she could take the rejection.

She threw back the covers on her bed and sank into her sheets. Kathryn walked in moments later.

"I'm tired."

"So you've said," Kathryn said. She crossed her arms and leaned against Angeline's closed door. "Charlotte is actually very nice."

"I'm sure she is. But I don't need you plucking people out of the wild to be my friend. That's weird and insulting." Angeline buried deeper beneath her blankets.

"I just thought we could use a buffer between us. We've obviously been at odds lately, and I don't want to leave lasting damage to our friendship. No matter what I do, it's wrong. I just can't please you."

"Oh, stop," Angeline said. "Don't be a martyr. It's fine. If you want someone else living with us, I don't really care. She seems like some sort of vampire groupie."

"That's not fair. She's not. Just give her a chance."

"I said fine."

Kathryn huffed and walked out of the room, shutting the

door loudly behind her. Angeline closed her eyes, but visions of her mother and the life she'd left behind so long ago played over and over in her mind like a film stock stuck on repeat. She hadn't stayed in Lowell after leaving the hospital. She'd taken a taxi right back to Boston, where she got a hotel room for the night. She couldn't bear the sights and sounds of her old stomping grounds, even though they'd changed drastically over the twenty-year period. It was too painful.

But Kathryn wasn't completely wrong. Even though Angeline resented her and scoffed at everything she tried to do, there were times when Kathryn seemed to genuinely want Angeline to be happy. But Angeline pushed it aside. She'd been brooding for so long, she forgot what happiness even looked like. Maybe having someone new around would change the dynamic enough to reconnect Angeline to a world she had so reluctantly left behind.

CHAPTER THIRTEEN

Fog Hollow, Massachusetts, current day

The cell phone on her nightstand vibrated loudly. Megan slapped at it a few times before knocking it onto the floor. She reached down and saw Detective Nolan's number displayed on the screen.

"Hello?" she answered, her voice thick with sleep.

"Megan? Nolan here. Would you be able to come down to the police station to have a quick conversation?"

Megan adjusted her eyes. It didn't even look like the sun was up yet. "Now?" she asked. She was fully awake by that point.

"I'd appreciate it, yes."

"Did you find something out about that night at the Gas 'n' Eats?" Megan asked, suddenly concerned for Angeline. Even though she was upset with the way they'd left things, she didn't want the police department anywhere near her.

"Why don't you just come down and I'll fill you in on what I'd like to discuss."

"Okay. I need a few minutes to get ready."

"Take your time," Nolan said before hanging up.

Megan's heart began to beat faster as she brushed her teeth and combed her hair. What could they possibly know that involved her in some way? All of the tests they had taken, along with the video, had ruled Megan out as a suspect. What could it possibly be that had to be done so early in the morning?

Throughout the drive over to the police station, Megan waffled between texting Angeline to let her know something was up or waiting until she was on her way home. As she was pulling into a parking spot, she decided that there was no reason to worry Angeline until she knew for sure that there was a reason to. It might have been completely unrelated. Doubtful, but maybe.

Prior to the gas station incident, Megan had never been inside a police station in her life. Except for that one time that her sixth grade class had baked cookies for the first responders of Fog Hollow and personally delivered them. Now it felt like her home away from home. Detective Nolan greeted her in the hallway.

"Nice to see you again, Megan. Come on back," he said, holding the door open to the small room with a couch and water cooler inside it.

Megan took a seat on the couch and clutched her bag to her stomach. Detective Nolan spread some file folders out on the table in front of him while pausing to sip his coffee.

"Coffee? Water?" he asked, holding up his mug.

"No, thanks."

"Thank you for coming. After what happened here a few weeks ago, I left Fog Hollow and returned to the city, wondering if this would be the case that would follow me throughout my career. You know the ones, the unsolved murders that haunt law enforcement. But once I was home, with my wife and daughters, I felt like I'd be able to let it go after all. Maybe there would be a break, maybe there wouldn't. And I'd be okay either way. Then, last night around dinnertime, I get a call from my boss, telling me that my assistance is needed in a small town out west. He thinks that I'm familiar with the town. It's Fog Hollow, and there's been another murder that he'd like me to investigate. Another murder. In a town that hasn't seen any real crime in more than a decade. The good officers here are doing everything by the book but feel like they may be a little out of their depth with this one." Nolan took a sip of his coffee and loosened his tie. "Now, I'm sure you can imagine my surprise."

Megan didn't know if she was supposed to interject or ask questions or what. Another murder? As horrifying as that was, in such a safe town, in *her* town, what did that have to do with her? She decided to just keep silent.

"Not only was another person killed, but their body was discovered just a mile from the Gas 'n' Eats. A guy taking his dog for a walk found him lying in the dirt just off of Cobblestone Court. Take a look," Nolan said, flipping open one of the folders and sliding it in front of Megan.

She gasped and covered her eyes before she could make out too many details. A man was lying on the ground surrounded by pine needles, his face contorted into a death mask. "Why are you showing me this?" Megan asked angrily.

"You know him?"

"He might look familiar, but I didn't get a good look and I'd rather not. Who is it?"

"Jud Jenkins."

"Doesn't ring a bell," Megan said. All she could see in her mind was the slack jaw, terrified eyes, and ghostly-white complexion from the photo.

"He was an employee at the Gas 'n' Eats. Worked the weekend shift. Officer Brent told me if the town had a drunk, he'd be it. Single guy in his sixties, liked his sauce. He's had a few DUIs in his time and a drunk and disorderly. Other than that, I come up empty. Why would anyone want to kill this man?" Nolan asked, finally closing the folder and pulling it back toward himself.

She was able to place him once Nolan identified him, even if the memory was hazy. "How would I know that?" Megan was starting to get anxious again. Did they really think she killed this guy? Not only the shooter from that terrible night, but Jud Jenkins? So now she was a serial killer?

"I don't know, Megan. But there's something real interesting about the way this guy was killed."

"Okay?"

"You want to see the photo again?"

"No!"

"Well, he appears to have bled to death. He has two puncture holes right in his left internal jugular vein. But there's not a drop of blood on the ground beneath him. Doesn't that sound odd to you?" Nolan tented his fingers beneath his chin.

The last time they had been together, Nolan had been much kinder. This time, he seemed sarcastic and agitated. Megan didn't like it.

"Yes, it does sound odd."

"Vampiric, almost?"

Megan sighed. Of course. "Sure, if vampires existed, it sounds exactly like something they would do."

"So now you're saying they don't exist? Everything you said to me when I was here last was all a lie?"

"No! I still can't explain it. I know what I saw and what she told me, but the more I thought about it, the less sense it made. You can't make me the bad guy because I told you exactly what someone else said, even if what they said was weird. I even gave a description to the artist person. I've done what you asked and told you everything." Megan shifted uncomfortably.

"Maybe. Or maybe you're hiding something."

"I didn't kill him!" Hot tears filled her eyes, more out of frustration than anything else. A vampire killing. Had Angeline killed someone and dumped them that way? She couldn't believe it. "When did it happen? I was working last night!"

"I'm not saying you killed him, Megan. But I think you know something."

Megan just shook her head weakly. She was afraid the more she said, the more she'd contradict herself. She couldn't unravel. Not now. She stood up to leave, and Nolan didn't stop her.

❖

Megan sat in the parking lot, fumbling in her purse for her cell phone. There was a missed call from Angeline. She hadn't left a message.

Are you still at work? Megan texted.

No. I'm parked across the street from you.

Megan looked up and saw the faint outline of Angeline's Mustang. She squinted to see if she could make out any of her features, but it was too dark.

Sorry to drag you out. I tried to keep my emotions in check, but I obviously didn't do a very good job.

It's fine. What's wrong?

Meet me at Burger Whiz.

Was she being tailed? Megan didn't know very much about real-life police procedure, but there were no other cars around. She decided meeting Angeline anywhere other than the police station parking lot was a good idea.

She watched as Angeline's headlights came to life and she pulled out onto the main road. Just seeing her car drive away stirred the butterflies in Megan's stomach, though she told herself it was just uneasiness of her meeting with the detective. She needed to put those feelings aside.

Burger Whiz was predictably deserted, as there weren't enough people craving a mushroom supreme before the morning commute for them to justify opening. Angeline was parked in a spot underneath a tree, her lights already off.

Megan pulled up next to her and jumped out of the front seat. She didn't see any cars nearby or any driving toward them. She heard the click of Angeline's doors as they unlocked for her.

"Hi," she said softly, sliding into the passenger seat.

"Hi." Angeline gave her a tight smile and played with the nail on her right thumb.

Being so close to Angeline gave Megan a rush of excitement mixed with sadness. She looked amazing, as she always did, in dark blue jeans and a form-fitting leather jacket. Her hair was down around her shoulders, and she wanted to reach out and touch her. Just for a second. Just to feel her again.

"So," Megan said, clearing away the sudden constriction in her throat, "I got a call from the detective a little while ago. He wanted me to come down and answer some questions about another murder."

Angeline's head snapped up. "Another murder?"

"Yes. Another employee at the gas station was killed. He had, um, two holes in his neck and his blood was drained. Like, all of it, I guess," Megan told her, watching as Angeline's eyes grew in horror.

She gripped her steering wheel, her expression going from horror to contemplative. "Who did it? Do they have any suspects?"

Unless she was a hell of an actress, it hadn't been her. Relief flooded her and she relaxed into her seat. "Sort of. They suspect me, I think, and you. But I told him that I must have been delusional to ever believe your crazy story and that I haven't heard from you since. I don't know if it worked."

Angeline shook her head. She reached over, took Megan's hand, and squeezed it. Megan squeezed back harder. She found herself desperate for Angeline's touch and she didn't want to let go. "You know I didn't do this, right?" Angeline asked, looking into Megan's eyes.

"Of course. I know you're not a killer. At least not in the usual sense of the word," Megan said. She still held on to Angeline's hand. Her skin was soft and receptive.

"It's a setup. Who else knows about me?" Angeline's phone chimed with a notification, and she removed her hand from Megan's to silence it. Megan's hand hung stupidly in the air when Angeline broke their contact, and she tried to brush it off by running her hand through her hair.

"Just Stacey and Kristen. I haven't told anyone else. Have you? Has there been anyone else since you moved here besides me?"

"No one."

Megan swallowed. "Is there the remotest possibility that it's a coincidence? Is there an animal that could have done this? Or some serial killer who thinks they're a vampire?" Megan knew how ridiculous that sounded before the words were even out of her mouth.

"I highly doubt it. In all my years, I've never heard of an animal that carefully removed the blood of its victim but left the flesh intact. That just doesn't happen. As for a serial killer, not only would that be insanely coincidental, but draining a human is a lot harder than you may think. And time consuming." Angeline looked out her window. "Unless the detective was bluffing. Maybe he was just trying to get you to confess to something? Or give me up?"

Megan shrugged. "I don't think so. But in all honesty, I didn't look at the photo very closely. I hid my eyes. Sorry."

"Don't be sorry. I probably would have turned away too," Angeline said, touching Megan's leg absentmindedly. "But the fact that there's a photo makes me think he wasn't bluffing. When did the killing take place?"

"Just last night, as far as I know."

Angeline creased her brow. "The medical examiner will perform the autopsy today, I would assume, so I don't have much time beyond that. I'll have to go to the ME's office tonight. Impromptu vacation day, I guess. Thankfully, the clinic shouldn't be too busy tonight."

"Wait, what do you mean? Why are you going to the medical examiner's office? To look at the body?" Megan asked, incredulous.

Angeline nodded. "I'll know by inspecting the victim whether or not it was a vampire bite. If it isn't, and Nolan's trying to draw me out, I may have to think about leaving town. There's just no way having someone on my scent could end well. It's easier to move on. And if it *is* a vampire bite, then we have a whole other problem on our hands."

"I'm coming with you," Megan said, watching Angeline for her reaction. It was just as she expected.

She shook her head. "Absolutely not."

"Why not?"

"It's too dangerous. If we get caught, it's over. I'll have to kill whoever finds us, and neither of us want that."

Megan sat back and pursed her lips. "I can be stealthy."

Angeline smiled. "I'm sure you can. But the answer is still no."

"I'll just meet you there then." She wasn't about to back down.

"You don't know when I'm going. So no," Angeline said.

Megan could tell she was trying to sound authoritative, but her twitching lips betrayed her. "I'll just camp out there for the night then. I assume the morgue has to have a back entrance, right?"

Angeline dropped her head to the steering wheel. "Again. I really, really appreciate you wanting to help, and wanting to look out for me. But honestly, Megan, there's too much risk and too much at stake. I promise I'll call you when it's over."

Megan touched her shoulder lightly. "Okay. You win. I'll stay home and watch *The Lost Boys* and wonder why you don't hang upside down in a cave like *those* vampires do."

Angeline closed her eyes for the briefest of seconds and then pressed the unlock button on her door panel. "Get out," she said, laughing.

Megan obliged, closing the door behind her. She waved, and Angeline held her hand up in return. She shivered as she turned the key in her ignition, and Angeline drove off as her car thundered to life. The feelings were still there, and they were blossoming instead of withering.

Why did everything have to be so damn dramatic in her life?

She couldn't just find a nice girl to maybe go see a play and have a late dessert with? No, she had to find herself infatuated with one she was going to surprise at the medical examiner's office. Even if she just stayed in the shadows, Megan didn't feel right leaving Angeline completely alone when there might be someone, or something, out there hunting her. Yes, she was nearly a hundred years old, and yes, she could snap the spine of just about anyone like a toothpick, but even she couldn't possibly account for the element of surprise one hundred percent of the time. As she pulled out onto the road, Megan knew she was going for her own peace of mind even as she justified needing to be there for Angeline. Angeline wouldn't even have to know she was there.

Chapter Fourteen

The ceiling fan hummed a comforting tune as Angeline stared at it, her body splayed like a rag doll on her plush sofa. She couldn't stop thinking about her. She'd done exactly what her head had told her to do. Push Megan away. Make sure she was perfectly clear that nothing could ever possibly progress between the two of them. Megan was vibrant, spirited, alive. Most importantly, *human*. And Angeline, she told herself, was basically a walking corpse. What kind of a future could they have? One where Angeline was constantly on edge because the weakness of humanity would leave her devastated and alone? *Again?* No, she wouldn't do it to herself. She refused to feel that deep anguish of loss that she'd felt all those years ago.

But something was tugging at her. Nagging her from the inside out. She could hear the tiny voice inside her head insisting, *it'll be different this time.* She was pretty sure she hadn't drunk that much coffee or eaten that much diner food in at least three decades. But those stolen moments and quick meetings were becoming the best parts of Angeline's days. Seeing Megan light up at the sight of a lemon poppy seed muffin in the wee hours of the morning was like feeling the sunlight on her face again. Hyperbolic, maybe, but she felt it in her bones. She was falling in love with her, damn it.

She could talk herself out of it. It wouldn't be so hard. She just needed to be rational about it. Love was just an illusion. The idea that one person was different from another, that one person could fill an imaginary void. That same rationale also told her that the surest way to turn Megan into a pleasant memory was to stay away from her. Put physical distance between them as well as emotional distance. But she was failing. Miserably. As much as she told herself that was what she needed to do, Angeline couldn't seem to manifest it.

Angeline jumped off the couch in a panic as a loud knock filled her living room. She stood still, seeing if whoever it was would just go away. Thirty seconds or so passed, and she calmed slightly as the threat seemed to have passed. Maybe it was a motorist or someone who'd gotten lost on their way to Lake Quinsigamond. Cell phones had all but eradicated the need for person-to-person contact in those situations, but there were still one or two reasons that someone would need hands-on help.

As she was about to turn toward the kitchen, another bang on the door set her on edge. Whoever it was, wasn't going away. Angeline walked slowly toward the door, her muscles tensing. Her eyes widened at the flashing blue strobing in her driveway. *What do they know?* Ignoring them wasn't really an option, since the soft glow of her lamp could be seen from the front porch. She took a deep breath and unchained the lock.

A young officer stood on her stoop, looking impatient. Angeline said nothing, just looked at him expectantly. She was ready to pounce on him if necessary.

"Good evening, miss," he said, nodding in her direction. His demeanor seemed to change as he addressed her. His impatience dissipated immediately. "We're just alerting everyone in the neighborhood to a possible gas leak. The construction crew over at the Hole-in-One Donut Shop hit a gas line. It's a good distance from here, so you should be fine, but I still wanted you to be on alert. If you smell any natural gas, you need to evacuate immediately."

Angeline nodded cautiously. Was that really it? Or was he

hoping to get her to drop her guard so he could lunge? "Will that be all?" she asked, half of her still hidden behind the door.

"Yes, that was it. If you need anything at all, we'll be over at the dig site."

"Okay. Thank you for the heads-up." Angeline smiled slightly and closed the door. The officer stood there for an extra few seconds before walking back to his car. He looked back at her house before getting into his car and driving away.

"Weird," Angeline said out loud to her empty house. She checked the time and decided to go get dressed for her busy night ahead.

Ever since she'd found out that Stacey and Kristen knew about her, she'd been waiting for the shoe to drop on her existence. Everyone would know, the whole town would show up at her door demanding answers and ready to burn her at the stake. She still couldn't explain what had made her tell Megan so much that night. It was a hasty, irresponsible decision that she somehow didn't regret. Megan wasn't the first person she'd saved from the brink of death. But she *was* the only person Angeline had stuck around for. It had been her protocol to do what she could without being seen and disappear into the shadows without confirmation of the person's condition. She didn't believe in fate, but something had made her stay. And now the loneliness that she'd become so accustomed to seemed at bay, parked in the recesses of her recent past. But not a part of her present. She found that she'd been happier in the last month or so than she'd been for a very, very long time. But happiness was fleeting, and Angeline was more than aware of that. So, she had to rein it in, suck it up, and distance herself from the very thing that was making her feel so alive. She just needed to force herself to actually go through with it.

CHAPTER FIFTEEN

"Ew," Megan said, stepping over a foul-smelling pile in the backyard of the house she was appraising. She checked the clock on her phone for the thirty-seventh or so time. Six thirty-three. She'd made all of her appointments late in the day so she could sleep in as late as possible. It was going to be a long night.

She took the last of the necessary photos and crammed all of her paperwork into the brown leather bag hanging at her waist. The leaves crunched beneath her feet, providing the perfect soundtrack to her heightened nerves. She wondered if there would be some kind of battle between good and evil, if there was a rogue vampire that Angeline would have to set on fire in the parking lot of the morgue. She felt guilty for being a little excited about the adventure aspect of the plan.

Once she was back in her car, Megan dialed Angeline's number. The lights were off in the large colonial she was appraising, so she assumed the family was out for the evening. Otherwise, making phone calls from their driveway would have seemed kind of odd.

"Hey," Angeline answered. She sounded like she was outside.

"Hey. What are you doing?"

"Drinking."

"Are you at a bar?" Megan asked. Angeline had never seemed all that interested in alcohol.

"Um...no. It's not really the best time to talk right now. Can I call you back?"

"Okay. You sure everything is all right? You're not drunk, are you?"

Angeline sighed. "Not that kind of drinking, Megan."

"Oh. *Oh.* Yeah, call me back." Megan quickly hit the end button on the call. Angeline must have been with someone satisfying her hunger or whatever it was that she did. She tried not to dwell too much on what that would look like. Knowing Angeline, Megan doubted that she would leave any lasting imprint on the...victim. She'd rather not think of them like that, but that's what they were. No sense in sugarcoating it. It would have been a lot easier for Angeline to just ignore Megan's call. Megan could lie to herself and say that she didn't glean a little satisfaction from the fact that she answered her call during...*that*, but really there was no point.

When she walked through her front door, Merlin greeted her like always. She gave him a quick pat and went into her bedroom to find the right criminal-activity-type outfit. Even if she ended up staying in the car, she still needed to be prepared. She decided on black jeans and a black sweater. Predictable, but smart. She assumed it would make sense to blend in as much as possible.

It had been a few weeks since the Pantsuit debacle, and Megan had texted with Stacey here and there, but she still held a little bit of a grudge over the way the events had gone down that night. It wasn't like she was never going to speak to her again or anything like that, but there was also a part of Megan that felt a little strange about certain elements in her life. Not embarrassed but guarded. She decided she was being silly. She and Stacey had been through plenty of ups and downs in their decade-long friendship. Stacey wasn't going to judge her over something as trivial as a pseudo-relationship with the undead. No, it was time to get over it, and if they were willing, to enlist Stacey and Kristen in the midnight charade. She could end up being stuck in the car for hours, and it would be a lot more enjoyable with someone to talk to. Thankfully, Stacey acted like no time had passed and everything was fine. Her ability to sweep things under the rug was one of the qualities that Megan loved about her.

"So, what do you think?" Megan asked, shimmying her ankle boots on over her thick socks.

"We're in," Kristen yelled from the background. Stacey had put her on speakerphone while Megan explained what had happened.

"I don't know, Meg. Wouldn't it just make more sense for her to, I don't know, go into hiding or something until they figure out who really did it?" Stacey was silent for a moment. "And have you considered the other possibility?"

"She didn't do it."

"I'm totally not saying she did. It just seems a little coincidental, don't you think? All of a sudden there's a vampire killer on the loose, just after the gas station nightmare where you meet a vampire?" Stacey said.

Megan could almost hear her chewing on her thumb. "It does. Which is why she wants to check it out. If it was a setup, then she can go into hiding or whatever until they close the case. If it really is another vampire, then apparently we have a big problem on our hands." Megan leaned back on her elbows and closed her eyes.

"We?"

"Angeline. So yes, we."

It was a revelation of sorts. As terrifying as the prospects of some unfriendly vampire in the town were, Megan realized that she wouldn't let Angeline handle it alone. It was fairly evident that Angeline didn't need her help, or particularly want it. She didn't want Megan to get hurt, or any more involved than she already was, which endeared her to Megan even more. The whole thing was ludicrous, really. She was probably unnecessary, extraneous, unwarranted, and most likely more of a hindrance than a help.

But that didn't change the fact that Megan wanted to be there for her. Even if they couldn't be more than what they were, Megan didn't want Angeline out of her life. Somehow, she had to make sure Angeline didn't need to leave town.

"Don't worry, Meg, we'll be there! We're totally going to help," Kristen yelled again. "Stace, stop being such a chicken. It'll be fun, and we owe it to Megan after the Tricia fiasco."

"Ugh," Stacey said. "Fine. But we're totally going to get arrested."

"You're not," Megan said. "We don't even have to get out of the car. She doesn't know we're coming. Exactly."

"What do you mean?" Stacey asked.

Megan could hear the suspicion in her voice. "She's said that she's fine on her own. And I'm sure she is. But I don't think it would hurt to have someone nearby who'd be on her side if everything went to hell. Seriously, as long as everything goes according to plan, she'll never even know we're there."

Stacey reluctantly agreed, but Kristin was all in, as usual. Megan texted Angeline one last time to confirm that she wanted to go it alone. Her phone rang immediately after she hit send.

"I'll be *fine*," Angeline said, drawing out the word.

"I know you'll be fine," Megan said. If her cell had a phone cord, she'd be twirling her fingers around it like she did in high school. "But I just wanted to make triple sure that you don't think you need someone there. Just in case."

"You do remember that I have certain skills that aid in that kind of thing, right? One of the few perks of being a creature of the night is my ability to hear and sense things. If someone is coming, I'll know about it long before anyone else will."

Megan sighed. "You're right. Please be careful." Guilt was beginning to creep in. She should probably just stay home and wait for Angeline to call her when it was all over.

"I will. This isn't that big a deal, I promise. I'll be in and out faster than the police could possibly respond to any alert they receive."

"Okay. Call me when it's over and let me know what you find out."

Angeline really would be fine without Megan there to muck up the works. But again, she was just going to sit idly by and make sure that everything went smoothly. Nothing wrong with that. She knew about Angeline's heightened senses, but she was still getting used to the whole vampire thing. It didn't just happen overnight. She ended the call and sat on the couch to wait while Merlin stretched out across her lap.

❖

Stacey and Kristen sat inside Stacey's Civic, the engine running to keep the heater going. Megan sat in the back, shivering in her sweater. Her only winter coat was a bright blue puffer jacket, and she didn't think that would be stealthy enough.

They were parked beneath an oak tree near the back of the building. Stacey and Kristen were chatting about a movie they were planning to see, while Megan fiddled with a zipper, her stomach the tiniest bit queasy.

Not much later, Megan saw a flash of black and brown come around the corner toward the side door. Megan could tell by the flutter of butterflies as well as the wavy brown hair flowing down Angeline's back that it was her. It was also late and only a crazy person would be creeping around a morgue. A crazy person or a vampire. She wondered if Angeline felt any of those tummy things at the prospect of seeing *her*. Other than her cryptic explanation of the two of them being incompatible, she hadn't said much of anything. But Megan was willing to bet that she hadn't imagined the way Angeline looked at her, or the way she'd reached out and touched her even though it was totally unnecessary.

"There she is!" Megan slapped Kristen on the shoulder and pointed.

"Where?" Kristen asked, whipping her head back and forth.

"Right there!" Megan said, pointing again. "Wait. I just

saw her there a second ago. Do you think she got spooked by something?"

"Probably by us. What did you think was going to happen?" Stacey asked, craning her neck to see behind her.

A loud knock on the car window solicited screams from all three of them. Megan jumped off the seat and nearly hit her head on the roof. She rolled down the window slowly, just enough to feel a blast of cold air hit her in the face.

"Really?" Angeline asked. She didn't sound pleased.

"I know, I know. Don't be mad. Please. I just wanted to make sure you were okay."

"And you decided to bring a small caravan of people to make yourself as conspicuous as humanly possible?"

"We're parked under a tree! At night! At a morgue! No one is around to be conspicuous *to*." Megan swallowed. She knew she should have just stayed home.

Angeline ran a hand through her hair. "I appreciate your concern, I do. But like I said, it's dangerous and you shouldn't be here. Please go home."

"Can't you just do what you need to do? You said you'd be quick. I'd feel a lot better if I could just see you walk away in one piece. Is that so much to ask?" Megan asked.

"We can go," Stacey said, and then clamped her mouth shut at Megan's boring gaze.

"Push over," Angeline said, opening the back seat door. "Scoot over."

Megan moved, unsure of Angeline's angle. How mad was she?

Angeline sat in the seat next to her and pulled on her sweatshirt strings. She seemed to have had the same idea as Megan, in her black jeans, black hoodie, and black sneakers. Megan gave her the once-over and raised her eyebrows.

"What? I'm fast, I'm not stupid," Angeline said.

Kristen whipped her head around and strained as far as her

seat belt would let her. "Hi! We've heard so much about you. It's so nice to finally meet you."

"Good to meet you too," Angeline said, glancing over at Megan.

Kristen was nothing if not obvious. "I don't mean to be a fangirl or anything, but I have *so* many questions for you. You are just as beautiful as Megan said you were. Is part of that the supernatural thing, or did you look like that as a human too?"

Megan cringed.

Angeline continued to smile. "Thank you," she said, casting another look at Megan. "This is how I looked back then, too. Probably a little softer."

"Just so you know, we would never tell anyone who you are, or what you are, or anything like that. You can totally trust us," Kristen said.

"I appreciate that. I'd hate to turn Fog Hollow into a bloodbath."

Awkward silence ensued. Megan gave Angeline a look and chuckled uncomfortably.

"Just kidding," Angeline said. "Too soon?"

Megan nodded. "Too soon." She turned toward Kristen. "She doesn't really do that kind of thing."

"No, of course not. Bad joke, sorry. Sometimes I forget that I'm basically a horror movie character and not just an introvert with a blood disorder," Angeline said. "I haven't been open around humans like this in, well…actually, never."

"Don't apologize," Stacey said. "This is new for us, obviously. If we thought you were dangerous, we wouldn't be here. I've been friends with Megan a long time. She's a good judge of character."

"If I asked you to turn me, would you?" Kristen asked, touching up her lipstick in the visor mirror.

"Kristen!" Stacey and Megan yelled her name in unison.

"What?"

Angeline laughed. She seemed to be lightening up. "No, I would not. Turning humans into vampires is not my thing. And it's a hell of a commitment."

"Have you ever turned someone?" Megan asked. It seemed so intrusive, but she couldn't help herself. Having Stacey and Kristen there to ask questions made it easier.

Angeline turned to her window. "Just once."

"Really? Just one time in a hundred years? Good for you. I'd be turning everyone. Family, friends, etc. No way would I face an eternity alone," Kristen said.

"Not quite a hundred, but I get your point. There are some advantages, but it's much more of a burden than a blessing. The hiding, the hunger, the fear, the loneliness…I'd never condemn someone I loved to this life."

Kristen prattled on for the next few minutes, but Megan caught Angeline's eye and gave her an appreciative smile. She was thankful for Angeline's graciousness toward her friends, even though she'd just completely disregarded Angeline's wishes. Kristen wasn't one to pull punches. When Angeline put her hand on the door handle to get out, Megan stopped her.

"Just let me go with you. I'm here, you're here, there's no one else here. I won't say anything, I won't interfere. I just want to be there for you. With you." Megan looked quickly toward Angeline and then at the floor. There was only one car in the parking lot, a white van with no windows. The squat brick building had the Massachusetts seal on the front door and an American flag mounted to the left of it. Megan felt her heartbeat quicken.

"You sure you want to do this? I'm completely against it, but if you really feel like this is something you need to do, I won't stop you," Angeline asked, leaning into her. Her warm breath tickled Megan's ear. "You don't have to. And I'd rather you wait here."

Megan just nodded and opened her car door softly.

"Okay. We're going to stay here, with the lights out,

obviously," Stacey said, pointing to the large hanging branch above them. "This provides decent cover. We'll text you immediately if we see anything. Megan, you have your phone?"

Megan patted her back pocket. "Yup. Set to vibrate."

"Good. Angeline, do you need us to do anything else?"

Angeline shook her head. "Thank you both. This is risky. If you two want to leave, I totally understand. Megan will just have to go with you."

"What are friends for?" Kristen asked, patting Angeline on the shoulder as she slid out of the back seat.

Angeline looked almost wistful as she got out of the car. They walked quickly toward the side entrance. Angeline shook her head. "I'm really upset with you, you know. You shouldn't be here."

"I know, and I'm sorry. I didn't mean to upset you, honestly. I was just worried."

Angeline looked toward her and nodded slightly. Megan gave her a small shrug of repentance.

There was a heavy metal door with a brass keyhole. It had a plastic sign nailed to it that read: NOT AN ENTRANCE. Angeline pulled a lock pick set out of her back pocket.

"You can't just, you know, kick the door in with your super strength?" Megan asked, bouncing up and down nervously.

"I probably *could,* but don't you think that would raise a lot more questions in the morning?"

"Good point."

Megan watched as she slid the long metal pick into the deadbolt and turned it over and over until they heard a distinctive click.

"I'm impressed," Megan said. "Where did you learn how to do that?"

Angeline smiled. "I had a locksmith friend back in the sixties. Which seems to be about the time period this lock was made," she said, nodding to the door. It opened easily, and Megan braced herself for the sound of an alarm. Angeline sighed when there was none.

"Wow, they're really lax with the security in this place. If you go into a big city, the morgue is like Fort Knox," Angeline said, closing the door behind them.

Megan just stood there, rooted in her spot on the linoleum floor. The smell of bleach and disinfectant assaulted her. There was a metal gurney stationed in the middle of the room, a lumpy white body bag with a black zipper lying on top of it. There was a line of stainless steel drawers lining the back wall, and Megan had seen enough crime shows to know exactly what they were. She shivered.

"You okay?" Angeline asked.

"I've gone from never seeing a dead body in my life to two of them in a very short time span," Megan whispered. "Well, I've seen bodies at wakes, of course, but I don't think that counts."

"Very different," Angeline said, rubbing the back of her neck. "You really don't have to do this. I know you just want to show support, and you're so amazingly sweet for doing that, but honestly, you should go wait in the car with your friends."

"No," Megan said, taking a deep breath. "I'm fine."

Angeline reached over and squeezed her hand. They stood like that for a second, hands grasped tightly. Megan squeezed back before letting her go.

"It's not this one," Angeline said, referring to the body on the table. "By now they'd have it in the freezer to prevent decomposition."

She walked over to the wall with the three drawers and glanced back at Megan before opening the first drawer. Megan nodded from a few yards away.

Empty.

"They don't have any hallways in this place? Just walk right in and, boom, dead bodies everywhere," Megan asked, looking around the room. The soft fluorescent lights cast a shadow over the numerous sinks and cabinets.

"We came in the morgue entrance. I'm sure the front door has a nice lobby and a reception desk and no dead bodies."

Angeline pulled the second drawer open and breathed out. Megan took a few steps forward but stopped when she caught a bluish-tinged leg out of the corner of her eye. She looked on in horror and Angeline dipped her head close to the body's face.

"What are you doing?" Megan whisper-shouted.

When Angeline came up, her eyes were wide and alight, and razor-sharp fangs replaced her bicuspids. She was both terrifying and beautiful. Megan gasped and stepped back toward the door. Any lingering doubts she might have had about Angeline's story were erased.

Angeline quickly turned away from Megan and slammed the drawer shut. "I'm sorry." When she turned back to her, her teeth had retracted, and her eyes had their normal honey shine instead of the preternatural glow. "I'm sorry," she repeated.

"No, I…" Megan trailed off, unsure how to finish her sentence. She was afraid, but the fear was dissipating now that Angeline looked normal. "It's not your fault. I know what you are."

"Knowing what to expect and actually seeing it are two very different things. The wounds and the smell on this body just made me…well, it doesn't matter. What matters is that there's a vampire in town that *isn't* me." Angeline shut the drawer tightly, the metal on metal reverberating through the silent room.

Megan didn't really understand the significance. Angeline was in town, and she was a vampire. So, really, what was one more? Angeline had gone all this time undetected, so it seemed plausible that another one could have done that too. Angeline came over, and Megan involuntarily flinched.

Angeline stopped in her tracks. "You're afraid of me now?" She looked like she was on the verge of tears.

Megan swallowed. She wasn't. Was she? "No, I'm not. I'm sorry. Just a little freaked out. I think it's this place more than anything."

A loud clang in another part of the office startled them both. Megan stood stock-still, as did Angeline. The phone in her back pocket vibrated loudly.

"Shit," she mouthed, slipping the phone out silently and holding it so Angeline could see the message.

A light just went on in one of the upstairs rooms! You have to get out NOW!

Megan shook her head as she returned her phone to her pocket. So much for an advance warning system. Angeline tiptoed toward the door as footsteps made their way down a set of stairs. Megan was torn between wanting to scream, throw up, or pass out. She'd never been arrested in her life, and now she was going to go to jail for tampering with a dead body. Or something like that.

Angeline pushed the door open slowly, cringing at every small creak. When the steps seemed to be coming in their direction, Angeline threw the door open and hoisted Megan over her shoulder. Megan grunted as her stomach hit Angeline's shoulder unexpectedly. The next thing she knew, a hollow voice was calling out "hello" from the morgue behind them while she was flying through the parking lot at a breakneck pace.

"Get in," Angeline demanded, dropping Megan at the back seat door to the Civic.

She didn't really comprehend what had just happened and the world was still spinning slightly, so she dropped into the back seat. Angeline was next to her before she knew it.

"You didn't hear anything?" Megan asked, facing Angeline as she buckled her seat belt.

"No. I was too engrossed in the scent left on him. It was exhilarating to smell that again, but not in a good way. I heard someone when whoever was up there was already on the move."

"Are you guys okay? We didn't see anyone walk in, I swear!" Stacey said, turning around.

"We're fine, just drive."

Stacey pulled out onto the main road with her lights still off.

Once they were a few hundred yards away from the coroner's office, she flipped her headlights on.

"My heart is still racing!" Kristen said, turned toward Megan and Angeline in the back seat. "What happened in there?"

Megan sat quietly, still absorbing what had happened. She wasn't sure how she felt about it all. Seeing Angeline next to her, looking the slightest bit insecure, broke her heart. Megan covered Angeline's hand with her own, rubbing her thumb over the soft skin.

Angeline squeezed Megan's hand. "We got what we came for. We wanted to know if the murder of that man was committed by a living person or a vampire. It didn't go the way I'd hoped."

"So, what does that mean?" Stacey asked.

"That means that his death was definitely caused by another vampire. Which leads me to believe that whoever did it is either trying to set me up, scare me off, or threaten me in some way. I just don't know the hows or the whys," Angeline said, looking out her window.

"Maybe it has nothing to do with you? Couldn't it just be that some other vampire stumbled into Fog Hollow and that gas station guy was vulnerable?" Kristen asked.

Angeline shook her head. Megan knew she'd already explained the unlikelihood of that scenario, so she probably didn't want to do it again. Angeline seemed edgy, much different from her usual laid-back demeanor. It must be serious.

"It's nearly impossible," Megan said.

"Why?"

Angeline sighed. "Honestly, it would be such a coincidence that I think I'd have a better chance of winning Powerball. There aren't many vampires in the world. It's nothing like you see on TV. And between the few of us that do exist, there's a kind of code, you know, you don't just go around killing people and drawing attention for no reason."

Kristen and Stacey exchanged a look. "How do you know that, though? If there aren't very many of you, how do you know that everyone got the memo outlining how they're supposed to behave?" Kristen asked.

"Vampires aren't born in a vacuum. We're created. Made. For different reasons according to the people who make us. Some want to continue their lineage, some want a lifelong companion, some just want to see if they can do it. But everyone has a maker, and it's that maker's responsibility to instill all of the age-old bullshit into their progeny. If word got out, and it would, that a vampire was creating baby vamps all over the place, they'd be hunted down. If they decided to go rogue, then someone, somewhere, would find them, and destroy them. There's no other way we could have existed for the last millennia if there were any indications that we were real. You know how people react to things they don't understand. They fear it, and then they kill it."

Sympathy flooded through Megan once again as Angeline spoke. She couldn't imagine living every day in such isolation. Even when Angeline was around people, she couldn't be herself. Ever. Even around Megan. Her reaction to Angeline's transformation had been normal, of course, prey reacting to a nearby predator, but that didn't take away from the idea that Megan had highlighted Angeline's differences, intentional or not.

"Who knows you're here? Besides us," Stacey said, squinting at the darkened road.

Angeline shrugged. "No one that I know of. I've been very careful covering my tracks, or so I thought. I never stay anywhere for more than ten years, usually much less. I leave nothing behind. I don't use my real name, and I never had a Social Security number of my own. I pay for everything in cash. I don't know how anyone would find me."

Megan bristled. "Angeline isn't your real name?"

"It is. I use a different last name. And sometimes I change up my first name too—Angela, Angie, Angelina, even Angel I think, once. But Angeline is my given name."

"You paid for your Mustang in cash?" Kristen asked.

"I did."

"You make that much as a vet tech? Really?"

Angeline smiled. "Of course not. I work there because I enjoy it. I've amassed a great deal of money over the years. I had a very lucrative partnership with an organized crime family in the eighties. They called me the Invisible Assassin."

"You killed people for the mob?" Stacey asked incredulously.

Megan just stared at Angeline, mesmerized and intimidated by how much she didn't know about her.

"Not very often. I don't like to kill anything. It was mostly to put the fear of God into them. That, I did. Turn here."

"Where are we going?" Megan asked.

"My place. The police are watching your house, I'm sure," Angeline said.

The thought of being watched, of her normal life being turned upside down that way, was panic inducing.

After a few more miles, Stacey pulled the Civic into a long driveway, so long that the house could barely be seen from the road. When it finally came into view, Megan marveled at the three-story log cabin. There were lanterns hanging from tall posts on either side of the front door, illuminating the walkway in warm light.

"This is where you live?" Kristen asked, her tone mirroring Megan's awe. It looked more like a resort getaway than a lived-in home.

"Yes. Do you two want to come in?" Angeline asked Kristen and Stacey, opening her door.

"Def—"

"No, we have to get home," Stacey interrupted, giving Kristen a look. "Meg, will you be able to get home okay?"

Megan looked at Angeline. Angeline nodded. "I'll take her home before dawn. Thank you both for your help tonight."

Angeline extended her hand, which Megan took. They could have taken her home, and it would just look like she'd been out with friends. But Angeline hadn't asked if Megan wanted to do that. The assumption that she'd be staying while her friends left was clear. She looked back at Stacey and shrugged. Stacey smiled and shook her head, backing slowly out of the winding driveway. Megan followed closely behind Angeline, the woods surrounding them acting like walls to keep the rest of the world at bay. Megan couldn't complain.

Chapter Sixteen

Averill Park, New York, 1953

September had been cold. Probably the coldest September that Angeline could remember. She looked out onto the lake, the moon reflecting in its shimmer, and a shiver coursed through her. She grabbed a pair of socks from her dresser and pulled them up as high as they would go. They nearly touched her kneecaps.

She climbed back into bed, pulling the covers up tightly. She nearly screamed as something icy cold touched her thigh.

"What is that?" Angeline whispered loudly.

Charlotte chuckled. "Sorry, my hands are freezing. I was trying to warm them up," she said, sliding her hand between Angeline's thighs.

"You could warn a girl, you know," Angeline said, sinking down to eye level with Charlotte. She kissed her gently on the lips.

"Where's the fun in that?" Charlotte asked. Her voice was full and throaty, and Angeline felt the implications of that between her legs.

Charlotte rolled over on top of her, her blond hair creating a curtain of privacy, where no one existed but the two of them. Angeline ran her hands up the length of Charlotte's back, about ready to make quick work of the silk nightgown she was wearing. Charlotte kissed her, this time without pretense.

"Knock, knock." A sarcastic voice interrupted them. Kathryn stood in the doorway, watching them with her eyebrows raised.

"Jesus, Kathryn!" Charlotte yelled, rolling off of Angeline and covering herself up to the neck. "I thought I locked that door!"

"You did," Kathryn acknowledged. "But sometimes I don't know my own strength." She shrugged.

"What do you want?" Angeline asked, pushing the hair out of her eyes. She was in no mood for Kathryn's passive-aggressive bullshit.

"I was going to take the boat out for a bit. I'm bored."

"So? Go do it, then."

"I'm not going *alone*, Angeline. I wanted you to come too," Kathryn said, folding her arms across her chest.

"Kind of busy here," Charlotte said, motioning to the bed. "I think we're all set."

Kathryn glared at her. "I don't remember asking you. I doubt the residents of this lovely town would take kindly to the two of you fucking in the middle of the lake."

"Okay," Angeline said, getting out of bed. "Enough. Kathryn, let's go in the other room for a minute."

"Seriously, Ang? Why do you always let her do this?" Charlotte said. She sounded petulant, but Angeline knew she was just frustrated. It wasn't the first time Kathryn had barged in on their private time.

"Exactly who do you—" Kathryn said, starting toward the bed where Charlotte was now sitting up.

Angeline could see the twitch of Kathryn's lips, which never meant anything good. "Stop." Angeline put a hand on Kathryn's chest, halting her mid-stride. "Let's talk."

Charlotte rolled her eyes and grumbled something, falling back to her pillow with a huff. Angeline continued to usher Kathryn out of the room and closed the door behind her.

"I've just about had it with her, Angeline. I mean it." Kathryn's eyes were enflamed.

Angeline didn't doubt her in the least, and Charlotte didn't seem to have the sense to be afraid. "I know. Sit. Let's have a cup of tea." Angeline went to the cupboard and removed two small teacups. Kathryn clearly fumed but took a seat at the dining room table anyway.

Things hadn't been good between Charlotte and Kathryn since they'd left South Carolina one year earlier. Not that they'd ever been great, really, but at least tolerable. Once Angeline had realized that Charlotte wasn't so bad, and she actually kind of liked her, Kathryn's attitude toward her changed. New York, which was Charlotte's home state, had seemed to grant her a fresh sense of confidence and poise that she hadn't displayed down south. She no longer acquiesced to Kathryn's every whim, and she had no problem putting her in her place. Angeline usually agreed with Charlotte, but there were times when even she cringed. It was as though Charlotte sometimes forgot that Kathryn was a centuries-old vampire with more power in her pinkie than Charlotte possessed in her whole body. Though that fearlessness was one of the reasons Angeline found herself so attracted to her, it was dangerous.

It hadn't taken long for the two of them to realize there was chemistry between them. Subtle glances, delicate touches, suggestive allusions. Charlotte finally told Angeline, when she could stand it no more and she had to do something about it. Angeline was adjusting the rabbit ears on the television when Charlotte came up behind her and knocked her to the ground. Angeline's instinct kicked in at the assault, her fangs detracted, and she was ready for a fight. But a fight wasn't what ensued with Charlotte straddling her, completely naked.

While it certainly wasn't accepted, two women together wasn't completely unheard of, either. There were clandestine gatherings and events that Charlotte sought out, trying to find a sense of community. Charlotte told Angeline that she had known who she was for a long time, and the second she'd laid eyes on Angeline, she'd known that she had to have her. Charlotte was the closest thing to that kind of love Angeline had ever felt.

Kathryn was fine with it, in the beginning. She'd make snide comments and make fun of them for being cutesy together, but she'd seen them as relatively harmless. She'd even told Angeline that it was the happiest she'd seen her in the last twenty-five years. And that it was a good look on her.

As time went on, Angeline found herself despising Kathryn less and less, mostly because she had a buffer. Charlotte was there when Angeline was grieving or melancholy, and instead of telling her to get over it, Charlotte would ask her about her family, about her life, and let her relive those experiences without feeling guilty about it. She no longer needed anything from Kathryn, and the freedom was blissful. She began to appreciate her for who she was—a bitter, entitled, insecure little girl trapped in the body of someone who'd lived too many lives for their own good. She wasn't without some merit. Kathryn took the bull by the horns and arranged everything for them—living quarters, income supply, vehicles, and whatever else they needed to blend in as ordinary citizens. Angeline knew that Kathryn had a soft spot for her, a love that was genuine, if often difficult. Even after their countless arguments and pointless fights, Kathryn always tried to make sure that Angeline wasn't angry with her.

"Why are you so on edge?" Angeline asked, taking a seat across from Kathryn.

Kathryn fidgeted with her necklace. "I think we need to make a clean break, Angeline. You've had your fun; you've been able to branch out a little bit. She's getting too headstrong for her own good. I don't like it."

Angeline tensed. "What do you mean, 'make a clean break'? In what way?"

"We'll just pack up and leave. You can write her a nice letter about how you enjoyed your time with her, but we had business to attend to in, I don't know, Athens." Kathryn shrugged like it was the most normal suggestion in the world.

"I can't do that. I don't *want* to do that." Angeline shook her head forcefully. She should have known that Kathryn would eventually try to take Charlotte away from her. If anything made her happy while simultaneously taking attention away from Kathryn, it eventually disappeared.

"Why not?" Kathryn asked defiantly. She stared into Angeline's eyes, taunting her. "I never said this was a permanent arrangement."

"Kathryn, she's been with us for almost five years. You know how I feel about her. I will *not* just pack up and leave her behind."

"How *do* you feel about her, Angeline? Tell me."

"I love her."

Kathryn laughed. "You love her because she's convenient. She knows what you are, she accepts it, and she's attractive. Moderately attractive, anyway. Frankly, she's a bit of a heel."

"Fuck you, Kathryn. You have no right to tell me how I feel, and your insults are a poor attempt to mask your own self-doubt. Or jealousy. Or whatever it is that you so poorly try to conceal. So again, fuck you." Angeline could feel the anger threatening to expose itself through her gums, but she needed to keep it at bay. She wasn't about to challenge Kathryn to any kind of physical duel, so it was better to just keep calm.

Kathryn waved her hand condescendingly. "It's adorable that you're so willing to stand up for your lady love, but can we please be serious here for a minute? We haven't gone to Texas yet. I hear their ribs are to die for. We could be ranchers or some-thing. Although I'm not sure how much ranching one can do at night," Kathryn said. She drummed her fingers on the table thoughtfully.

Angeline opened her mouth and then clamped it shut. And then repeated the action. Was Kathryn toying with her on purpose, or was she actually being serious? "I'm not sure if I made myself clear enough. I. Will. Not. Leave. Charlotte. So you can get that idea right out of your head, Kathryn. It's not going to happen."

"Won't it? You're familiar with the Bible, of course. Job chapter one, verse twenty-one, to be exact. Except you can substitute my name for 'The Lord' since even *I'm* not that arrogant. But the meaning remains. Kathryn giveth and Kathryn taketh away. I'm giving you the opportunity for one final kiss-off. This chapter is ready to come to a close." Kathryn smiled, the tips of her fangs showing.

Angeline stood up so abruptly her chair skidded backward into the cabinet beneath the sink. "Maybe you're right, Kathryn," she said. Her body betrayed her and released her fangs. "Maybe this chapter is ready to be over. Maybe this was just Book One, the Kathryn Chronicles. And now, maybe it's time for me to branch out without you. Write a whole new story that doesn't even include you."

Kathryn was up in her face before Angeline could finish her sentence. Their faces were so close their fangs nearly touched. "You will never leave me, Angeline. That isn't how this works. You think you have free will and are able to come and go as you please? You belong to *me*. I found you, I created you, and if the time comes for us to no longer be together, then I will dismiss you or I will kill you. Do not mistake my kindness for weakness. Just because I indulge you and allow you to live as you see fit doesn't mean that I'm not your lord and master. Now go into that bedroom, tell that woman that it's over, and I expect that she'll be gone by morning. If not, I'll make her gone." Kathryn's voice was low and guttural. Angeline knew that it was time to toe the line. She didn't want to find out what would happen if she crossed it.

She turned away. "Fine. You win, as usual. I'll go talk to Charlotte. It's not going to go well, so I need some space. Why don't you go take that boat ride, and I'll go tell her," Angeline said, tears springing to her eyes.

Kathryn's demeanor relaxed immediately. She smoothed her hair down and cleared her throat. "It's for the best, Angeline, really. I know you don't see it right now, but you will. I don't like to hurt you, you know that. But I've been around a lot longer than you."

Yeah, right. You don't like to hurt me. But instead of saying anything, Angeline just nodded.

"Okay, honey. I'll go out for a while. Don't be sad. There'll be many more Charlottes along the way, believe me. Remember Roger back in Mount Pleasant? I liked him a lot. He really did it for me, if you know what I mean. But hey, Rogers are a dime a dozen. So are Charlottes. You just need to remember to keep your heart out of things, and you'll be fine. See you in a bit." Kathryn blew her a kiss and took her handbag from the kitchen counter.

Angeline watched her leave with a mixture of derision and dread. She stared out the window until she saw the boat float away from the dock, swaying gently in the no-wake zone. She couldn't really ask Charlotte to leave. That wasn't an option. But if she didn't, Angeline feared for her safety. She slammed the side of her fist onto the kitchen table and yelled "fuck" angrily.

Charlotte opened the bedroom door and leaned on the door frame. "What happened?" she asked quietly.

"She's just irrational. Maybe a little psychotic. I don't know." Angeline wasn't sure exactly how much to share with Charlotte. She didn't want to cause her unnecessary panic. Or maybe it was necessary to get Charlotte to understand the danger she was in. Angeline hadn't been in that kind of situation with Kathryn before. She'd never actually cared for a woman beyond one night.

"Of course she's irrational and psychotic. You're just figuring that out now? I've known that since the day she invited me to your home in Charleston," Charlotte said, an amused smile playing at her lips. "What did she say? She wants us to leave? Is she finally tired of playing third wheel?"

Angeline sighed. "Something like that. She wants us to

leave. Me and her. Apparently, the trio thing isn't working for her anymore."

"Excuse me?" Charlotte said, storming into the kitchen. "You told her to piss off, right? Where is she, anyway?"

"She went out on the boat. She'll be back in a few hours."

"Good. At least she can't use her stupid vampire ears to eavesdrop. Did you tell her we'd be happy to pack up and go? I can be ready in an hour."

"It's not that easy, Char," Angeline said, sitting at the table. She covered her face with her hands and rubbed them up and down vigorously. "She won't just let me go. Kathryn would rather see me dead than happy without her. If you're not gone by the time she comes back, I'm afraid she'll try to hurt you." She paused, closing her eyes. "No, not hurt you. She'll kill you. I don't know what to do. I'm no match for her, Charlotte. She's physically stronger than me in every way possible."

Charlotte walked over to Angeline and rubbed her shoulders gently. She kissed the top of her head. "Then we'll just vanish. If we take the Buick, we could be in Vermont in just over an hour. We'll find a remote place to camp out for the day, and then we'll hit the road at sundown. Think about it. We'd be in Canada in no time. She'll never find us there."

It sounded good. Better than good. It sounded fucking amazing. Angeline covered Charlotte's hand with her own, trying to decide if that plan would even work. Kathryn's senses were heightened, more so than Angeline's, but if they had an hour lead time, she couldn't possibly track them that way. Right? She'd have to resort to old-fashioned methods like phone calls and driving. Extreme speed was great in small bursts, but it certainly didn't last for a hundred miles. Once they were in rural Canada, it would be hard for a bloodhound to pick up their trail, never mind an enraged vampire.

"You're sure you want to do this?" Angeline asked, standing to face Charlotte. "Before we met, you were a city girl. If I'm going to run from her, I'll need to stay hidden for a long time. A *long* time. Years. You really think you'll be happy living in some hovel we'll have to build ourselves, out in the middle of nowhere?"

Charlotte held Angeline's face. "If that hovel has you inside it, I'll be happy there." She kissed Angeline lightly on the lips, and then drew her in for a hug. Angeline held on to her tightly, sure of her feelings for Charlotte but unsure if they were making the right decision. If Kathryn found them, she'd kill them both without hesitation.

"Come on. Let's go throw a few things together and hit the road. I could use a Vermont cheddar omelet for breakfast." Charlotte kissed Angeline again before disappearing into the bedroom.

Angeline breathed deeply. She looked out the window to see if she could spot Kathryn's boat, or any sign of her on the horizon. The sun wouldn't be up for a few hours still, so they had some time to put distance between them and Averill Park. Resolve strengthened, Angeline met Charlotte in the bedroom and began stuffing clothes into a duffel bag. She went into the bathroom and took all of her toiletries from the shelf. Angeline was almost giddy with excitement. She'd accepted her lot in life, as Kathryn's companion, and she'd even found slivers of happiness here and there, but the idea of total freedom was so very enticing.

"Should I take some food? I suppose I can grab something at a gas station once we hit the Vermont border." Charlotte plucked a sleeve of crackers from the cabinet and added it to her handbag. "Can you fit my rollers into your bag? Mine's totally full."

"Really?" Angeline asked, smiling. "We're running for our lives and you're worried about hair curlers?"

"Being a fugitive is not an excuse for unkempt hair, my darling. Shove them in."

Angeline picked up both of their bags and brought them out

to the Buick. She checked the lake again for any sign of Kathryn, but the water was still and silent. No sign of a boat cruising back toward their dock.

"Don't forget the playing cards!" Angeline yelled toward the house. She slipped the key into the engine to let it warm up for a few minutes. She blew into her hands to warm them up, the September wind unforgiving on such a cold night.

Would she miss Kathryn? Maybe a little. They had, after all, spent the better part of two decades together. There were weeks where they'd barely say two words to each other, and other times they'd hit the town, dance, laugh, drink, and have a wonderful time together. Those times didn't make up for Kathryn's possessiveness or mean streak, but there was still a tinge of nostalgia there.

Angeline looked impatiently toward the house. What was taking her so long? She wondered if Charlotte understood the gravity of the situation. If Kathryn came back and found them packed and heading off without her, she would be enraged. Angeline wasn't sure exactly how pissed she would be, but she didn't want to find out. If Angeline hadn't wanted to keep quiet, she would have beeped the horn. She checked the gas gauge and was happy she'd filled it just the other day. They had plenty to get them to Vermont.

Finally, the porch door swung open. Angeline turned to see if Charlotte needed any help, but instead was greeted by a wild-eyed Kathryn.

"Going somewhere?" Kathryn asked, wiping blood from her bottom lip.

Chapter Seventeen

Fog Hollow, Massachusetts, current day

"Can I get you something to drink?" Angeline asked, standing in front of her refrigerator. "I don't have much. Some orange juice and some Sprite."

"No, I'm okay," Megan said, browsing Angeline's massive bookshelf. She had everything from the classics of Shakespeare and Tolstoy to the autobiography of Cyndi Lauper. It was obviously custom built, as it took up an entire wall.

"I like to read," Angeline said, startling Megan by coming up behind her. "I've had a lot of time on my hands over the years."

Megan nodded. "I can imagine. You have quite the array of tastes," she said, nodding playfully to a book about Miss Piggy.

"I do. For a while there, I was having ten to twelve books a month shipped to my PO box. That was in my recluse phase, I think. They add up quick. Hey, I found a couple of beers in my crisper. Any interest?" she asked, handing Megan a Coors Light.

"Definitely," Megan said, downing a huge gulp. "Mmm. I needed that. So what do we do now?"

Angeline shrugged. "I can take you home in a few minutes if you want. Or, you know, you could stay until sundown. I'm sure you're tired too. Is Merlin okay by himself?"

Megan felt a twinge in her stomach. Had Angeline just asked

her to sleep over? Even if she meant it platonically, it still sent a surge of excitement through Megan's body. "Yeah, he'll be fine. He's an independent guy. I left plenty of food and water, and the radio is set to golden oldies, so he's probably enjoying the solitude. I am pretty tired, now that you mention it." The last time Megan had pulled an all-nighter was during Bush Jr.'s first term. She yawned at the thought of it.

"Good. Do you want to sit down for a few minutes and finish our drinks? I could use a minute to unwind." Angeline motioned toward the leather couch, situated below an exposed beam.

Megan sat against one of the arms, her body sinking into the plush fabric. "Ooh, I like this. How did you find this little slice of heaven, anyway?"

"It was advertised in the newspaper as a wooded getaway house, probably for people who live in the city to escape to. Once I saw the pictures, I fell in love. I made an offer over the phone, paid the guy with a bank check, and voilà. Home sweet home." Angeline kicked off her shoes and put her feet up on the coffee table.

"Wow. I went through a *lot* more paperwork for my house." Megan laughed. Her smile faded as she thought about the body in the morgue. "So, tell me. Do you really think you're being hunted by another vampire?"

"That's my guess," Angeline said, sighing heavily. "I don't know what other kind of message a drained body could possibly send. Either they want to drive me away from this town or they want to hurt me. I can't imagine what else it could be."

"Do you know many other vampires? Any that would have a reason to be pissed off at you? Or that might want to take your spot in Fog Hollow?" Megan asked, cricking her neck back and forth. She wondered if the tension was manifesting itself in her muscles.

"No. The few that I've met along the way have only been acquaintances at best. I've kept my distance from nearly…

everyone. Here, turn around," Angeline said, making a spin motion with her finger.

Confused, Megan turned her body and felt Angeline's fingers push into the muscles above her shoulders. She nearly collapsed at the instant relief they provided. "Oh, you don't have to do that. But if you don't stop, I won't be mad."

Angeline chuckled. "I don't mind. I just have to stay on my toes. Vampires can usually sense one another in close proximity, although it's not all that hard to cover up the triggers. Cover yourself in pine scent and walk softly and that does the job fairly well. Usually only newish vampires walk around brazenly."

Megan was listening, but the way Angeline was working her shoulders was elevating her to a new plane of existence. Megan stifled a gasp when Angeline pulled the neck of her sweater back so she could touch her skin directly. Megan closed her eyes, telling herself that Angeline was just being nice. She knew Megan's neck hurt, and she was being helpful.

"You smell like vanilla," Angeline said, nearly in a whisper.

"I know."

Angeline's hands stopped moving, and Megan had to refrain from telling her to keep going. She was about to fix the neckline on her shirt and turn around, but Angeline's fingers trailed up from Megan's shoulder to the nape of her neck. She traced circles around the sensitive flesh of Megan's collarbone and the space beneath her ear. Megan shivered involuntarily at her touch.

Her eyes still closed, Megan felt Angeline pull closer, so close that she could feel her chest against her back. Instead of fingers, Megan felt soft lips caress the shell of her ear. Her heart sped up and pounded heavily against her chest. Angeline was touching her, and there was no mistaking her intentions. But why? She'd made it clear that they shouldn't explore that side of a relationship, it just wouldn't work. But the more Angeline's tongue caressed Megan's skin, the more coherent thought abandoned her. She couldn't take it anymore. Megan turned and saw Angeline's eyes level with hers. They were full of want. Angeline reached out and grabbed her gently by her hair, tightening her hand into a fist. She nudged Megan forward, their lips meeting in a burst of energy. It started out gentle and tender, but quickly turned desperate and unforgiving.

Instead of putting the brakes on and asking what the hell was going on, as she knew she should have, Megan's entire body responded to the kiss and she felt as though she were perched on the edge of a cliff, teetering on loose soil. Her hands tangled in Angeline's waves, pulling her closer, so close that they could melt into one.

Angeline pushed Megan back against the couch, where her head rested against the plush armrest. Megan groaned as Angeline molded herself to every one of Megan's curves, their bodies touching in every place imaginable. Angeline's lips trailed from Megan's lips to her neck, to her collarbone. Megan held her breath for what she envisioned would come next, but Angeline pulled away suddenly. She jumped off the couch as though something had burned her.

"What's wrong?" Megan asked nervously, sitting up.

"I'm sorry," Angeline said. She threw her head back and raked her fingers through her hair. "I never should have done that. I know I'm sending you mixed signals—"

Rage surged through Megan's veins. She bolted off the couch and stood face-to-face with Angeline. "*Mixed signals?* Are you fucking serious?"

Angeline looked taken aback. "I know, I was totally out of line. I'm sorry, really I am."

"No, fuck that, Angeline. Fuck *you*." Megan pressed her finger against Angeline's chest. "Why are you like this? You obviously want me as much as I want you, but you're a complete coward. Because we're *different*? You know what? Lots of people come from lots of different backgrounds and they're able to make it work. Would this be unconventional? Yes, of course! But I'm willing to give it a try, because I like you, and I'm attracted to you, physically and emotionally, and I want to see where this goes. But *you*. You just want to walk away and say, 'oh I can't, I'm tortured and sad,' but you won't tell me *why*. I've loved once and can never love again? That's bullshit, Angeline. Bull. Shit."

Angeline stood there, her mouth agape. If she were being honest, Megan was a little surprised by her own outburst. But that didn't lessen the truth of anything that had come out of her mouth. She was angry and excited and turned on and fuming all at the same time. Angeline's unwillingness to explore their potential, when she clearly wanted to, was infuriating.

"I like you, Megan, I *really, really* like you, and that scares the hell out of me. It's been a very long time since I've felt this way about someone, and I can't do it again. I just can't. Where are you going?"

Megan grabbed her jacket from where it was draped over one of Angeline's chairs. "Why not?"

"Why not what?"

"Why can't you do it again? Tell me. Help me understand."

Angeline drew in a breath but said nothing. She closed her eyes.

"That's what I thought," Megan said. "If you decide that you want to act like a grown-up and have a real conversation, you know how to find me."

She fought tears, because the last thing she wanted to do was cry. *Not now, not now.* Before she got very far, Megan felt herself thrust against the natural wood of the wall next to Angeline's bookcase. Her feet dangled as she hung suspended in air.

Angeline stared at her, her eyes glowing and her teeth sharp and pointed. Megan could feel the emotion dripping from Angeline's pores. She held Megan tightly by the shoulders. Megan trembled, though the pit of fear that swirled in her stomach wasn't as strong as it probably should have been. *She won't hurt me.*

"I'm a monster, Megan. I'm not some hometown girl with a secret or a mysterious stranger that turns out to be a princess. I am a *monster*. I feed on human blood and I've killed more people in my time on this earth than you've dreamed about. Doesn't matter if it was because I wanted to, or because I had to, or because someone else made me do it. If you think I'm some fairy tale villain with a heart of gold, you are sorely mistaken. I'm a killer, Megan. A killer. And being anywhere near me is dangerous."

Megan swallowed as she saw Angeline's eyes well up. It was hard to reconcile what was happening. She was being pinned to a wall by a woman who could rip her throat out as easily as she could shake her hand. But the sadness, the humanity, in Angeline's eyes drowned out any fear she might have had.

"I'm not afraid of you," Megan whispered.

"You should be, damn it! You need to be! *Be afraid of me!*" Angeline yelled, her voice gravelly and broken.

"I'm not afraid of you," Megan repeated. Angeline set her down gently and cried out in frustration. Megan cupped Angeline's face and looked into her shining eyes. Her teeth had retracted. "I'm not afraid of you."

Angeline leaned forward and kissed Megan, hard and furious. Megan kissed her back openly, silently pleading with her to know how much she'd meant what she'd said. She *wasn't* afraid of her. She didn't know if it had something to do with their blood bond, if it even worked like that, but for some inexplicable reason, she didn't fear the enigmatic vampire that continued to invade her every sense. She wanted Angeline, all of her, and she was willing to risk everything for just the possibility.

Angeline slid her hands down the back of Megan's thighs and lifted her like she was weightless. Megan wrapped her legs around Angeline's middle, while keeping contact with her lips. She was pretty sure she'd never been this aroused in her entire life.

The light that bathed the cabin in a soft glow seemed to fade in and out as Angeline carried Megan to her bedroom, where she laid her gently on the fuzzy black comforter. Megan grasped the back of Angeline's neck, pulling her down on top of her. She was afraid that if she let her go, Angeline would disappear, and Megan would wake up to find this had all been a dream. She couldn't bear to chance it. Angeline parted Megan's thighs with her knee, opening them enough that she could slip between them, their bodies fitting together like they'd been waiting centuries to discover that one piece of the puzzle that would complete their own abstraction. Angeline leaned down and kissed Megan again, softer this time, as though she were requesting entry instead of demanding it.

Her lips parted and Megan tilted her head to allow Angeline full access. The mutual desire felt like a liquid bubble surrounding them, threatening to pop at the slightest provocation. Everything else forgotten, Megan retreated from the warmth of Angeline's mouth and dragged her tongue lightly over the curve of Angeline's neck. She heard a moan escape Angeline's lips, which only goaded her more.

Strengthened by her excitement, Megan rolled Angeline onto her side and climbed on top of her, straddling her.

"Mmm," Angeline said in response. She grabbed a fistful of Megan's shirt, tugging on it. When Megan made no move to remove the offending item of clothing, Angeline sat up and raked her nails down the length of Megan's back, tearing the shirt in two. Megan gasped as she slid it down the front of her and tossed it to the ground like a flimsy hospital gown.

"I liked that shirt," Megan said, unable to contain a smile.

"I don't care," Angeline replied, pulling her down forcefully. She kissed Megan again, rubbing her hand up Megan's back, her touch on Megan's bare skin setting the kindling in Megan's stomach ablaze. She found the clasp of Megan's bra and undid it with a quick flick of her fingers. She flipped Megan again, so that she was lying beneath her. Megan looked up, aching for her. There was the slightest hint of fear, which she knew had absolutely nothing to do with the ivory fangs hidden beneath Angeline's gums. She wasn't afraid for her life. She was afraid for her heart.

Angeline seemed to sense a change, and she kissed her lips lightly. She ran her hand over the swell of Megan's breast, and her eyes flickered with pure want. "You are so beautiful, Megan. I've wanted you from the moment you opened your eyes that night in the parking lot. I don't think I've ever wanted anything so much in my entire life."

Megan swallowed, drowning in the thickness of the air that surrounded them. She grabbed on to the hem of Angeline's shirt, which Angeline shed immediately. They kissed again, flesh against flesh, tongue against tongue. Megan couldn't breathe, couldn't think. She felt like her entire body was on fire, sizzling at Angeline's touch. She felt like she was intoxicated, the way her head swam. But there was no way half a beer could have done that. It was all Angeline.

Angeline grunted in frustration at the button on Megan's jeans and Megan decided she couldn't wait any more. She grabbed Angeline's wrist and thrust it down the front of her jeans. The look in Angeline's eyes made Megan's stomach drop. Sultry. Ravenous. Unstoppable. She felt Angeline's middle finger trail softly up the length of her. Testing her, almost. A rush of breath escaped her mouth, followed by Megan clenching Angeline's hair in her fist.

"You're sure you still want to do this?" Angeline asked, her voice nearly unrecognizable. Megan closed her eyes as Angeline's tongue skated from the hollow of her throat, up to her neck, the rhythm matching that of the hand inside her pants.

"Shut up and take me," Megan whispered breathlessly. She covered Angeline's hand with her own and pressed on her firmly. Megan moaned as Angeline understood her encouragement and slid the fabric of her underwear to the side. Megan clutched the blanket and arched her back. Angeline took advantage of her position and pulled her jeans off easily. Megan tucked her fingers into the sides of Angeline's jeans and tugged, hoping she would take the hint so she could finally feel her body against her. She did and kicked them off in a flurry. She quickly resumed her position on top of Megan, and Megan thought she might float out of the room while Angeline kissed every inch of exposed skin. She removed the rest of their clothing without Megan even realizing it.

The wherewithal to be embarrassed had fled a long time ago, so Megan moaned and clawed at the sheets with abandon. She had never, *ever* experienced this kind of attention before, and it was slowly driving her mad. She was squirming submissively beneath Angeline's touch, wanting to hurry her but also wanting it to last forever. Angeline continued her journey southward, her left palm gently gliding over Megan's chest. She slid her finger down the length of Megan's wetness and slowly inserted herself as Megan cried out. She gripped the sheets with both fists, her body rocking with Angeline's movements inside her. Angeline brought her thumb up and began stroking her in slow, measured circles, keeping rhythm with her thrusts. Megan could feel herself getting closer, closer.

Megan lost herself completely before any coherent thought could be expressed. She grabbed on to Angeline's wrist, where her hand was cupped around her breast, and just gave in. Her orgasm crashed through her as she writhed against Angeline's fingers, oblivion swallowing her whole. Megan's whole body went weak with release, and she wondered for a second if she was going to pass out. Angeline slowly slid her fingers out when the aftershocks had subsided. Before she opened her eyes, Megan shuddered as the tingling gradually dissipated.

Angeline slid up beside her, softly kissing her shoulder and chest, rubbing her stomach lightly. Megan pulled her close, their slick bodies sticking to each other.

"I just saw literal fucking stars," Megan said. She laughed, shaking the cobwebs out of her head.

Angeline laughed too. She rubbed the pad of her thumb along Megan's jawline and kissed it softly. "We can just relax if you want to."

Megan was up on all fours in an instant, leaning her face into Angeline's, her knees at Angeline's sides. "Not a chance," she said, kissing Angeline fervently, with a desperation she had never felt. She could hear Angeline moan beneath her lips, as she rocked into her, their wet heat creating a volcano between them. Needing more, Megan trailed her way down Angeline's body, taking her breast into her mouth, teasing, licking, before traveling down once more and kissing the softness of Angeline's thigh. She sucked in her breath when she allowed the gravity of what she was about to do sink in. Angeline lay there, ready for her, so beautiful and vulnerable, so open and wanting. Softly, Megan ran her tongue up the extent of her, her stomach clenching with every twitch and shiver that coursed through Angeline's body. She felt Angeline's hands tangle in her hair, making it even more intense, which wasn't even possible. She stroked Angeline softly with her tongue, featherlight until Angeline couldn't take it any more and she heard her murmur "please." Wanting desperately to make her feel as good and as whole as Angeline had made her, Megan gripped her thighs tightly and concentrated on tight, slow circles, delirious in the taste of her. Angeline began breathing heavily, saying Megan's name softly, over and over, until it reached a crescendo. Angeline pulled hard on Megan's hair as the tidal wave hurtled into her, through her. Megan stayed, making sure she extracted every bit of pleasure that was to be had, until Angeline finally fell backward, spent and limp.

"Oh my God," Angeline groaned, covering her eyes with her forearm. "I don't think I will ever be able to walk again. Come here."

Megan smiled, trying to ignore the fluttery feeling in her stomach. She crawled her way back up to Angeline's mouth, where they kissed again, lazy and comfortable. Angeline kicked back the covers, cocooning them under her soft comforter. "Stay with me," she whispered, laying her head on Megan's chest. Megan stroked her hair softly enjoying the haze of sleep already surrounding her, ordering herself not to analyze what any of this meant.

Chapter Eighteen

Averill Park, New York, 1953

Panic flooded through Angeline's body. She felt as though she couldn't breathe. Kathryn continued her slow stride toward her, confident and condescending. Angeline regained her senses and flew toward the house, pushing Kathryn out of the way.

"*What did you do?*" she screamed, tearing up the steps in one giant leap.

Angeline ran toward the bedroom that she and Charlotte shared, wild-eyed and desperate. What she saw was worse than she'd imagined. Charlotte lay on the floor, her body bent at an odd angle. Blood streamed from the gaping hole in the side of her neck, creating a maroon pool in the shape of a sickening halo around her head.

"Ohmygodohmygodohmygod," Angeline cried, falling to her knees. She heard a slight gurgle come from Charlotte's throat. She felt her neck with two fingers and was able to find a weak pulse, barely enough to register through Charlotte's skin.

"You're going to be okay, Charlotte. I can save you," Angeline said. Her voice was thick with fear and her eyes were blurred with tears. She forced her teeth to retract and sank them into her own wrist to draw blood. She covered Charlotte's mouth with her wrist and pinched it to drive the blood out faster.

"Drink, please drink. Swallow. Come on, Charlotte," Angeline demanded, unaware at first that Kathryn had stepped into the room.

"I wouldn't," Kathryn said. The indifference on her face was infuriating. She had her hands on her hips and looked down at Angeline like she was watching a game of checkers.

"I don't give a fuck what you would or wouldn't do, you soulless fucking monster!"

"Well, don't say I didn't warn you," Kathryn said, shrugging.

Angeline ignored her, compelling Charlotte to swallow just one more time. That would be enough, wouldn't it? She hadn't ever turned a person before, but she was sure that her blood wouldn't be able to heal Charlotte; she was too far gone. Her only hope was that if she died with Angeline's blood in her system, she'd come to, and she'd transform. Angeline left her wrist in place while she hung her head and prayed—something she hadn't done in twenty years—unsure if it would be welcome or blasphemy.

Charlotte sputtered one last time, Angeline's blood trickling out of her mouth. She was dead. Angeline brushed her hair from her face, crying and pleading with her to wake up. "Please. Please," she repeated over and over. "Wasn't it enough?"

Kathryn nodded slowly. "Definitely. She'll wake up in no time."

"Kathryn, why did you do this? Why? *Why?*" Angeline asked, her desperation overwhelming. She didn't understand. She knew Kathryn was selfish and jealous, but she had no idea that she could be that cold, that hollow. Even at her meanest, Kathryn had never done anything so calculated.

"Dammit, Angeline, you know why! I told you to get rid of her or I would, and what do you do? You plan to run away, a little lovers' rendezvous, as though I would just *allow* that. I gave you a chance to send her on her way, which, might I add, was *extremely* generous of me. And you took that generosity and stuffed it down my throat like a sock doused with kerosene. So you can take all of your indignation and fuck off, Angeline, because *you* killed this bitch, not me."

Her mouth refused to move, to form any type of sound. There were no words to respond to Kathryn, no feelings that could sum up the rage and the fear and the disbelief that crowded Angeline's brain. Next to her, Charlotte's body twitched.

"Charlotte? Can you hear me?" Angeline asked, momentarily forgetting Kathryn behind her. Charlotte's body twitched again. And then she sat up so fast Angeline recoiled in surprise.

"No, no, no!" Charlotte screamed. She clawed at her skin. She thrashed backward, slamming her head onto the hardwood floor. "Make it stop! Oh, God, please make it stop!"

Angeline stood up in horror and turned to Kathryn. "What's happening? Kathryn, why is she like this? Kathryn!"

She sighed, but the glint in her eyes was pure evil. "I told you not to do it. True, I drained her of most of her blood, but I didn't want to leave just bones and skin. So I replaced what I took. With cyanide."

"You did *WHAT*?" Angeline yelled, raking her hair with her hands. Charlotte continued to writhe on the floor, screaming and flailing in deepest agony.

"It burns! Angeline, please! Please! Make it stop!"

Kathryn shook her head slowly, in mock concern. "If only you'd listened. Lots of lessons learned today, Angeline."

Angeline had never felt so helpless, so defeated, so desperate. "Kathryn, please! Tell me what to do! How do I stop it?"

Kathryn disappeared from the room and quickly reappeared with her steel katana that she kept mounted over the fireplace. "Go ahead, Angeline. Relieve her." Kathryn handed the sword to Angeline and nodded to where Charlotte struggled on the floor.

Angeline's eyes widened in horror. "No! I can't! I don't want her to die! I was trying to save her."

Kathryn tightened her lips and raised her eyebrows. "Then

let her suffer. I assume that she'll die anyway, eventually, maybe, but you can certainly take that risk if you'd like. This is a first for me too."

Blood dripped from Charlotte's eyes, mingled with her tears of agony. She whimpered and groaned, punctuating her wordless pleas with bloodcurdling screams.

"Do it, then!" Angeline yelled, backing up against the wall. "I'm so sorry, Charlotte. I'm so sorry."

Kathryn took a few steps toward her and held the braided rope of the katana handle out toward Angeline. "You do it. This is your mess, you need to clean it up."

Angeline wondered for a moment if she was on the brink of losing her sanity. Charlotte was a quivering, bloody mess on the floor before her, Kathryn was demanding that she kill Charlotte in an act of mercy, and only moments ago she was packing the car to leave for a quaint motel in upstate Vermont.

She had no choice. Charlotte looked to her, pleading for an end to the torment. Angeline took the katana in her trembling hands and Kathryn stood against the dresser with her arms folded.

"I...I can't..." Angeline stuttered, terror overwhelming her. But she had to push it down, she had to be strong. The killer that she so delicately harbored within herself emerged, ready to perform the horrible deed. Charlotte choked, a spray of blood cascading toward the floor.

"I love you," she whispered, and she held the sword above her head with both hands. She wasn't sure if she had hallucinated it, but she was almost certain that Charlotte nodded, giving her permission.

With a guttural cry, Angeline brought the sword down with every shred of her strength. Charlotte's cries ceased immediately, and the katana stuck in the wood floor beneath her head. The sword fell to the ground with a shattering clang as Angeline dropped to her knees beside it. She couldn't look at her. She couldn't acknowledge what she'd done.

"End it, Kathryn. Just end it. Please," she sobbed. "You can start fresh. Find someone new. Just fucking end me."

"Absolutely not. Don't be so dramatic. I didn't come this far with you just to send you into whatever afterlife lies beyond this nightmare. I know you're upset with me. It'll fade, I promise. The good news is that you're already packed. We should get going before anyone comes knocking to see what the racket was all about."

Angeline's sob caught in her throat. Her sadness and self-pity faded from her slowly, like paint running down a canvas. All that replaced it was fury. Whatever misguided loyalty Angeline had felt toward Kathryn was gone, any appreciation, any inklings of affection, any empathy toward her plight. Gone, gone, gone.

"You're right," Angeline said, standing up. She picked up the sword and stabbed it into the ground, leaning on it like it was a cane. She used the palm of her hand to dry her cheeks. She cricked her neck back and forth. "I was foolish to let feelings get in the way. It could only end this way. I never should have let it get as far as it did."

Kathryn flinched. It was a flashing micro-expression that flitted across her face, but it was there, and Angeline saw it. It only fueled her rage.

"Right. I'll throw a few things together myself and we can be on our way. I don't like the cold though, as you know, so I'd prefer we head back down south. Or maybe out west. I don't really care either way—"

Kathryn whipped around, but it was too late. Angeline speared her stomach with the tip of the sword and pushed forward at lightning speed until Kathryn was impaled against the heavy oak door leading to the outside. Kathryn grasped at the handle of the sword sticking out of her stomach, but she was weakened by the foreign object mingling with the power of her blood. Her eyes glowed like a cat's eye while blood seeped out like tears.

Her fangs dug into her lips with an anger Angeline knew she was trying to harness. She stared at Angeline with a horrible wonder.

"How could you?" Kathryn asked weakly, still trying to remove the sword from her stomach. It was lodged firmly within the thick wood. "I gave you new life. I protected you. I took care of you. I loved you."

Angeline scoffed loudly, her vision blurry through the darkness and tears. "*Loved* me? You've never loved anything in your life, Kathryn. If that's what you want to call it." Angeline watched as Kathryn struggled, unable to find purchase on the slippery handle of the blade. For the first time, probably ever, she felt no mercy. She felt nothing. "I despise you."

Angeline walked away from her, ignoring Kathryn's grunts and screams of frustration. She picked up the apothecary bottle that housed the long matches they'd used to get the fireplace going.

"What are you doing?" Kathryn asked, her tone wary.

Angeline sensed that Kathryn might actually think she was serious, and this time, she'd show no hesitation. No mercy. She rubbed the match along the striker, her lips curling back from her teeth as the flame engulfed the blue tip. As much as she wanted to remove the sword from Kathryn's stomach and behead her with it, she didn't think she'd be able to go through with it. Not again. Not so soon. And not to someone who would plead for their life. Besides, the slightest wrong move could put Kathryn back in control. At least impaled, Kathryn was unable to summon the strength to free herself.

"I'm granting myself freedom, Kathryn. The freedom that you've taken from me, over and over again. The freedom that I've allowed you to take. No more." Angeline grabbed a swath of fabric from the sheer curtains hanging in the living room window. She held the match to it and watched with fascination as the flame tickled its way toward the top of the curtain. It caught faster than she had expected it to.

"No. No, no, no!" Kathryn yelled, trying once again to pull

the sword from her abdomen. "You can't kill me, Angeline. You're not evil. I know you can't do this."

"Watch me." Angeline felt her fangs retract as she opened the kitchen slider. She looked behind her and caught a glimpse of Charlotte's shoe, the black sole facing her from its eternal resting spot.

"I'll kill you, Angeline. This is your last warning. I'll find you, and I'll break you so badly that you'll beg for the mercy of death. Let me go and I'll let you live. I'll let you go." Kathryn's voice was low and cracked, her eyes dangerous and desperate.

Angeline stood in the open doorway, watching as fire began to take over the wall like a spreading stain. She looked at Kathryn, who gripped on to the handle of the sword like she was willing it to release itself from the oak.

"Burn in hell, bitch."

The void of everything she'd lost suddenly swirled in Angeline's stomach like a twister. She ignored Kathryn's screams and curses and settled in behind the wheel of the Buick. The motor started up with ease and she cranked up the radio, so loud that the Andrews Sisters' rendition of "I Can Dream, Can't I?" rattled the Buick's speakers. She checked her rearview and saw billows of smoke heading up toward the night sky as though they had a destination in mind. She'd set herself free. Now she just had to set her course.

CHAPTER NINETEEN

Fog Hollow, Massachusetts, current day

The soft melody of Roy Orbison's "I Drove All Night" floated through the bedroom to Megan's ears. She opened her eyes and focused on the wooden planks of the ceiling. The black room-darkening drapes were drawn, so the only wisp of the light came from the shell-shaped nightlight plugged in across the room.

It was real. She'd dreamed of the night she'd spent with Angeline, and a small part of her wondered if that was all it had been—a dream. But no. Here she was, lying on a cloud of comfort, while her vampire lover was presumably in the other room. Possibly drinking blood. Maybe hanging upside down. There were still a few things that remained unclear. Megan jumped out of the bed and reached for her shirt.

"Right," she said softly, seeing the back torn in two. She felt desire begin to creep through her again before she opened one of Angeline's drawers and pulled out a T-shirt. It was an oversized green tee that showed Smokey the Bear warning about the dangers of forest fires. Just when Megan was sure Angeline couldn't possibly get any more adorable. She threw it on and went out to find her.

"Hey," Angeline said, standing from her place on the couch. She extended her hand, and when Megan took it, Angeline pulled her close. She kissed her softly. "I hope I didn't wake you."

"No," Megan said, tucking her hair behind her ear. "What time is it, anyway?"

"Almost two."

"In the afternoon?" Megan asked. She hadn't slept this late since her teens.

"Yup. I don't think we fell asleep until almost six. Thankfully, the sun goes down a lot earlier this time of year. It's a drag for me in the summer." Angeline fell back on the couch and pulled Megan down next to her. "Cute shirt."

"Thanks," Megan said. "Mine seems to be ruined."

"Sorry about that. Heat of the moment and all."

Megan laughed. "I know. Believe me, I'm not upset about it. One shirt was well worth the price of admission."

"Are you hungry?" Angeline asked, smiling.

"Not right now. I'll take your car and run out and get us a couple coffees in a little bit. I have GPS." Megan put her hand on Angeline's knee and rubbed it up toward her thigh. Being able to do this so freely made her want to jump up and down. But before she let herself get too excited, she had to get the heaviness out of the way. "So. What made you change your mind? You seemed pretty adamant that you didn't want to take this any further, and then you just kind of…did?"

Angeline shook her head. "I never *not* wanted to. I tried to make that super clear. I didn't think it was a good idea. I've been hurt. I've hurt people. Being with me can be a bit more… dangerous than you might think. Loving someone gives other creatures power over you, if they want to take it. I just resigned myself to the notion that I was better off alone. And someone that I actually cared about was better off without *me*. No matter what my heart tried to tell me."

"How long has it been?"

Angeline paused. "A really long time."

Megan raised her eyebrow. This would never work if Angeline insisted on being so secretive. It wasn't like she was the only person in this world to ever experience heartache.

"It's been, I don't know, sixty years, maybe," Angeline said, obviously taking her point.

"Sixty years?" Megan nearly yelled. "I thought you were going to tell me five or six or something. Wow, that is commitment to self-punishment. You haven't been with anyone in sixty years?"

"I didn't say that," Angeline said, smirking slightly.

After the night they'd shared, Megan didn't want to think about Angeline doing that with anyone else, sixty years or not. Maybe that was a minefield better left undetonated.

"Okay. But in an actual relationship?"

"Right. My last one didn't end so well. And rather than put myself, or anyone else, through that again, it just made sense for me to close off that part of myself forever. It's pretty easy to stay unattached, really, once you decide that's what you want. Until now, that's worked."

Had Angeline just suggested that they might be heading for a relationship? Sure, it was maybe too soon to make that call, but it hadn't felt like just sex. Megan felt elated that those feelings hadn't only been on her end. She couldn't help the warmth that filled her chest, knowing that she had been the one to break a six-decade-long pledge to remain alone.

"Did she leave you? Did you leave her? Was she a vampire? What happened?" Megan asked.

"She died," Angeline said, matter-of-factly. "She was murdered."

Megan recoiled. "I'm so sorry, I had no idea. I shouldn't have pushed."

Angeline shook her head. "Of course you didn't know. I'm not upset. It was a long time ago. I just carry a lot of guilt about that night, along with the knowledge of what love costs, which is why I don't really like to talk about it. She was killed because we were together. A good amount of the blame for her death falls on me."

Megan stayed silent for a second. Angeline's resistance to something more than platonic between them was slowly coming into clarity. No wonder she didn't want a relationship. "You mean like a hate crime?" Megan asked.

Angeline gave her a small smile. "No, not at all. We were very discreet back then. Had to be. Kathryn decided that Charlotte, who was a human companion living with us, was taking up too much of my time and attention, so she had to go. I refused and planned to leave that night with Charlotte. To get away from Kathryn completely. Just sever all ties. But I should have known better. Kathryn was not the type to let something like that happen. She had a pulse on everything around her. She found out and then she drained Charlotte to within an inch of her life. I tried to bring her back, but Kathryn had poisoned her, so then I had to kill her. I killed her to make the pain stop."

Megan bit her lip. She didn't know what to say. Telling Angeline it wasn't her fault sounded hollow, and saying she was sorry was too trite. Maybe she shouldn't say anything at all.

"Logically, I know Kathryn was the reason she died, but I still can't help that haunting feeling that I murdered her. If only I'd done as Kathryn said and let Charlotte go. I remember it all too clearly." Angeline shuddered. "After that, I just sort of snapped, and I killed Kathryn for what she had done. For what she'd made me do. I couldn't live under her thumb anymore. That was by far the worst day of my life. And in some ways, the best, as sick as that sounds. She's equal parts a distant memory and a constant participant in my nightmares. Even after so much time has passed. But it reminds me of the kind of creature I never want to become, no matter how much time has passed."

It sounded more like a movie than anything that could happen in real life. Megan reached out and clasped Angeline's hand, grounding her to the fact that Angeline was real, and she wasn't living out some fever dream. "Kathryn was your maker, right?"

"Right."

"I thought a maker was supposed to be like some sort of mentor, not a warden. It sounds like she tortured you."

Angeline sighed, running her fingers absentmindedly over Megan's palm. "She did, in a lot of ways. I have some good memories of her. But the bad far outweigh the good. I've been without her longer than I was with her, but I still feel a catch in my throat when another vampire is nearby. It doesn't happen often, but the handful of times I've sensed one over the last sixty-odd years, I feel that jolt of fear even though she's dead. At least, I think she is. I didn't stay to watch her burn."

Megan climbed on top of Angeline, straddling her on the couch. She leaned down and pulled her into her, so that Angeline's head was resting on her chest. Megan played softly with her waves. Angeline tightened her arms around Megan's waist.

"I can't even believe the things you've been through. It's all so surreal. I understand why you've been so hesitant to open up to anyone. I hope you don't feel like I pressured you into this. Whatever this is," Megan added quickly.

"Mm," Angeline murmured, placing soft kisses on Megan's chest, through the thin fabric of the T-shirt. "This feels amazing. *You* feel amazing. I've been afraid for too long. The pull I've felt toward you had little to do with our blood bond. I've wanted you so badly there were times I thought I was going to explode. I'm grateful that you persisted. Because really, what's the point of all of this if I don't allow myself to feel? And you feel so fucking good."

Angeline pulled Megan down forcefully, so that their bodies were melded together. She kissed her neck, her jawline, and finally landed at her lips. Megan was pretty sure that she felt lightning bolts exit through her fingertips as she draped her arms around Angeline's neck and deepened the kiss.

The shrill chime of Megan's phone jerked them both out of their haze of lust. Megan chuckled and pushed Angeline's hair behind her ears. "I should see who that is."

"Ugh," Angeline groaned, digging her fingers into Megan's hips. "Really? Now?"

"It could be my aunt, or the detective. I don't need an APB

put out on me. That would probably kill my appeal as an appraiser who has to go into people's houses and interact with the public. Hello?" Megan rolled off Angeline and answered, just before the call went to voice mail.

"Hello, Megan. It's Nolan. Are you at home?"

Megan felt the blood drain from her face. She hadn't really expected him to call. She cleared her throat. "No, I'm actually with a friend right now. Is there something I can help you with?" She tried to make her voice sound as casual and calm as possible. She wasn't sure what kind of a sentence messing with a dead body in a morgue carried, but she was pretty sure it was more than just a slap on the wrist. Angeline moved closer, like she was listening to the conversation.

"Okay. We're going to need you to come back in. We have another situation on our hands, and until you produce that 'friend' of yours that whisked you away from the crime scene at the gas station, you're the best lead I've got. I hope you feel like talking."

Another situation? What could that possibly mean? "With all due respect, Detective, I've told you everything I know. I had nothing to do with the gas station robbery and nothing to do with Jud Jenkins. Should I hire an attorney at this point? I don't know what else you want from me." Megan closed her eyes and hoped that the threat of lawyering up would cause the detective to back off. She knew that they had nothing on her besides her strange testimony of the vampire who rescued her.

"That's up to you. It'll make things harder on both of us, but I wouldn't try to talk you out of it. I'd rather you just come on over for another conversation without turning this into a pulling teeth situation. But again, the choice is yours."

Megan sighed at his poorly masked indifference. "Fine. I'll come by in a little while. But really, I have nothing new to tell you. So, I hope you're ready to hear a whole lot of I don't knows."

"Maybe you'll surprise yourself. I'll see you shortly."

Nolan clicked off the line, his patience apparently wearing thin. Megan was angry at him, but also at herself for having ever put herself in the position of being suspicious. She should have kept the whole insane vampire thing to herself until she figured out what was really going on. Angeline shouldn't have told her the truth that night in the parking lot. It was too much information that Megan didn't know what to do with and couldn't share. Angeline probably should have healed her and run off, leaving her at the crime scene so there weren't more questions than answers. At least her *I don't knows* would be genuine. She couldn't have known that she would end up falling for the vampire, but everything would have been a lot easier if she hadn't been so effusive at their first meeting.

"Man, he won't let up." Angeline frowned.

"He wouldn't tell me what this new situation is. But seriously, what else could it be? Did someone transform into a bat behind the police station?"

"You know that's not really…"

Megan shot Angeline a look. "Yes, I know that. Thank you. But this is getting out of hand. What if they give me truth serum and I lead them right to your cabin?"

"Pretty sure that's against the law. And there's actually no such thing."

Megan sulked.

"I'm sorry they're badgering you. Maybe I can go talk to him. I could come up with a story, something that would at least get him to back off you for a while."

That idea didn't sit well with Megan. She knew that Angeline was just trying to help, but it couldn't possibly end well. "What if he wants to fingerprint you? Which he will. Can you do that hypnotize thing and just make him forget about me?"

"No," Angeline said. "It's a quick trancelike state that leaves details foggy and memories unclear. All he'd have to do is go back to his desk and pull out the file to remember the players in the investigation. And he'd resume where he left off. I'd have to come up with one hell of a story and hope he'd buy it."

Megan could hear the doubt in Angeline's voice. Of course

that wouldn't work. "And if he doesn't buy it, and arrests you for tampering with evidence or evading law enforcement, or something along those lines?"

Angeline sighed. "Then it would get ugly. But what am I supposed to do? Just sit back and let him harass you because I was sloppy? I know better."

"You *did* save my life. So, there's that," Megan said, shrugging. "I don't want you to do anything hasty or stupid just because I'm a little inconvenienced at the moment."

Angeline scoffed at her minimization of it.

"I'm serious," Megan said.

"Okay, we won't do anything rash. Once we figure out who's doing this and put a stop to it one way or another, he'll leave you alone. Presumably. Or, if you want, we can go someplace else for a while."

"Together?" Megan asked. She wished she could pull the word back just in case she was reading too deeply into it.

"Yes, of course together. Unless…"

Megan nearly laughed at their awkwardness. "No, that's what I thought you meant, and I'm glad that's what you meant." She leaned in and kissed Angeline on the lips. "I'll go see what he wants and then we can decide what to do."

"Sounds like a plan." Angeline swung the key ring in a circle with her index finger. "Try to make sure you're not followed. If it looks like you are, simply turn around and go back home."

"Sure. Let's go get ready. We need to leave as soon as the sun sets. Are you working tonight?" Megan asked, picking her jeans up off the bedroom floor.

"No, it's my night off. I need to get this vampire bullshit squared away so I can get back to my quiet life of dog walking and cat petting," Angeline said. "Are you working?"

"Yes, but I can do it later. I don't have any appointments, just paperwork."

Angeline nodded, and Megan watched as she pulled some clothes out of her drawers and headed into the bathroom. It felt as though she'd been waiting forever to be with Angeline, but at the same time, it was all such a whirlwind. It was all so normal, and so freakishly different that the juxtaposition made her dizzy. Megan shook her head to rid herself of an ill-timed relationship analysis. There would be plenty of time for that later.

CHAPTER TWENTY

Angeline pulled up a little way down the street from Megan's front door, but her house was in view, as was the unmarked police car clearly sitting out front. Full dark blanketed the sleet-covered street. Megan smiled as she saw Merlin sitting in the window, licking his paw. Even amid the murders and robberies and otherworldly beings she'd been introduced to, Megan couldn't help but feel like all was right in the world. She leaned over to Angeline, who was smiling softly at her.

"Call me when you're done with Nolan," Angeline said and kissed Megan fully on the lips. "I'll watch from here to make sure you get in okay."

Megan's stomach dropped once again. She could get used to this. "I will," Megan whispered against her lips. She kissed the tips of her fingers and headed up the street toward her house. She ignored the urge to give the people watching her house a wave. No need to antagonize anyone. The night around her was still and serene.

"Hey, buddy," Megan called. Her cat came running into the kitchen, twisting around her calves and purring. Megan scratched his head. "I think you're gonna like her."

She filled his bowl with dry food and refreshed his water before opening a can of pâté. She grimaced at the smell, but Merlin was licking his chops before she even got it down on the plate.

Megan grabbed her laptop and stuffed some of her paperwork into a messenger bag just in case she ended up over at Angeline's again. She'd have to ask her about bringing Merlin over or else they'd need to spend more time at her place once she was sure that she was no longer under surveillance. There was something so calming about being tucked into the woods, just the two of them, with no one around for miles. Megan had always assumed remote living would terrify her, but Angeline brought such unexpected comfort. Such safety.

The ancient answering machine on the table in her foyer was blinking. She was pretty sure she was the only one left in town who still had a landline and an answering machine, but Aunt Susie favored her home number, so Megan couldn't bring herself to cancel the service. Sure enough, Aunt Susie's voice filtered out from the muffled speaker.

"Meg? It's me. I just wanted to check in on you. I haven't heard from you for a while. Your story is playing on the news again. Channel Five, I think. They went over everything again, but they also said there is still a question about what really happened that night. And they put up a number on the screen for people to call. Has anyone called? That boy shouldn't have been doing what he was doing, but to have his throat ripped out! And they still haven't caught the person who did it. Anyway, please call me and let me know you're safe. It's Aunt Susie."

Megan nodded, smiling. No matter how long she talked into the machine, Aunt Susie always had to make sure Megan knew who was calling before disconnecting. As though she had tons of elderly relatives blowing up her phone line.

"They *haven't* caught them, have they?"

Megan gasped and jumped back, colliding directly with another body. She turned and came face-to-face with a drawn-looking woman, her face gaunt and pale. The woman smiled but it didn't reach her eyes. Her expression was empty and frightening.

"Who are you and what are you doing in my house?" Megan asked, backing away.

"I think you know who I am. I can smell her all over you, so I'm sure you've heard the stories. The big bad villain who took everything from her. I never saw it before, but she always was an ungrateful bitch," the woman said, shaking her head.

Megan's voice caught in her throat and fear made her knees weak. It couldn't be. "K-Kathryn?" Megan whispered.

"In the flesh."

"But you're dead. Angeline said—"

"On the surface, that's an accurate description. But I'm sure that's not how you meant it." Kathryn grabbed Megan's hand, brought it to her nose, and sniffed before she dropped it disdainfully. "Ah. She'll be here soon if that blood bond is worth its weight in salt. I assume this house has a basement?"

Megan swallowed. Kathryn couldn't possibly have shown up to make amends or for any other reason that wouldn't end tragically. Could she? At least they knew who'd killed Jud Jenkins. Fear snaked its way up Megan's throat. "Is there something I can do for you?"

"Not directly. The basement?"

"Why do you need to know where the basement is?" Megan asked. She took a few steps backward, trying to seem casual. If she could just make it to the door, maybe the element of surprise would work in her favor. If she could wave to the police car outside...

"Because we can't do this in front of a picture window." Kathryn turned her head. "I assume it's through there," she said, nodding toward the door off the kitchen. She was right, damn it.

"Angeline?" Megan asked, squinting at the window beyond Kathryn's shoulder. Of course, there was no one there, but she couldn't think of anything else that might interest Kathryn enough to make her move.

It worked. Kathryn spun toward the window, her long red hair whipping behind her. Megan turned and ran toward the front door, cursing herself for installing a deadbolt in such a safe town. What used to be a safe town, anyway. She turned the grip of the lock and it clicked over, granting her access to the outside world. She reached for the doorknob as Kathryn sped toward her unnaturally, eliciting a scream from Megan that she didn't even know she was capable of.

Kathryn grabbed Megan's hair and pulled her back into the living room forcefully. Her teeth were glinted, and her shining eyes meant business. "Cute. Get down on your knees."

Megan could feel her resistance slipping away, which fueled the panic in her chest. "Just tell me what you want!"

"Oh, Christ. I don't have the patience for this."

Before Megan could ask what that meant, she felt a sharp blow to the back of her head and watched as the world faded to a charcoal gray.

CHAPTER TWENTY-ONE

Meredith, New Hampshire, 1954

It had been nearly a year since Angeline had left New York, broken and alone. She admired the black canvas of the night sky, speckled with more stars than she could ever remember seeing before. This early in the season, she had the in-ground pool to herself. The early June evening was warm, but not quite warm enough for swimming. Tourist season in the Lakes Region would pick up in maybe a week or two, but the motel had provided Angeline with a perfect short-term rental solution in the meantime. The owners, a nice couple in their sixties, were out the door by six o'clock each night. They'd left her their phone number in case of an emergency.

In the first few days on her own, Angeline had nearly succumbed to the panic of being alone. Utterly and terrifyingly alone. But as time marched on, she realized that maybe she'd been more afraid of the unknown than of actually being alone. Because being alone didn't seem all that bad.

The ability to make friends, or even acquaintances, had been abandoned in the nineteen twenties. And in her current condition, Angeline didn't think that a mixer at the local watering hole would be the smartest idea.

But an existence without Kathryn was easier than Angeline

thought it would be. She'd been afraid that she'd have all kinds of existential questions that could only be answered by someone with a lifetime of knowledge and experience. She found that she didn't have any, really. She'd been nervous that her nights would be filled with silence and she'd end up staked, surrounded by torches in a hunter's front yard because of her weaknesses and lack of skill. But that didn't happen, either. She'd been able to stay under the radar quite easily, and Lucy and Ethel had ended up being better company than Kathryn had been.

She still thought of Charlotte often, but the crying had finally stopped, and the guilt had subsided just the tiniest bit.

The sound of rustling behind her lounge chair made Angeline jump. She was on her feet in seconds.

"Miss? I'm sorry to have startled you. I was wondering if you had anything to eat. I'm making my way up to Canada, Montreal to be exact, but I'm about to go ape if I don't get some food. Everything around here is closed, even the gas stations."

The man spoke so rapidly, it took Angeline a moment to digest what he was saying. He was young, maybe twenty, with slicked-back hair. He had on black trousers and a loud Hawaiian shirt. Times had certainly changed. She could remember when a proper man wouldn't leave the house without a tie around his neck.

"I don't really have much," she said. "I think there may be a can of Franco-American spaghetti in the lobby. There's a small cupboard and a hot plate for guests that are passing through."

"Oh, thank you, I'm jazzed. If you'd offered me a bowl of week-old clam chowder, I think I'd take it. Phil's the name."

Angeline smiled as Phil followed behind her toward the motel entrance. She had a key, in case something happened after the owners had gone home for the night. They deducted fifty cents from her weekly rent for her generous availability.

It would have been easier to tell him to buzz off, or maybe take a quick drink for herself before sending him on his way.

But Phil seemed harmless enough, and she really ought to make conversation here and there if she wanted to at least fit in with society somewhat.

Phil sat in one of the faded wingback chairs while Angeline poured the contents of the can into a small saucepan.

"Now, I hope you don't mind me saying so, but you're a real doll. Are you circled?" Phil asked, flicking the ash of his Lucky Strike into the ashtray next to him.

"Excuse me?"

"Circled. Spoken for. You know, married."

"Oh," Angeline said. It was like he was speaking a foreign language. Every generation's slang got stranger and stranger. "No, not married."

"What are you doing here on your own?"

"Enjoying myself. I appreciate the quiet." She unfolded the tray table and set it in front of him. She placed the bowl of bright orange spaghetti down next to a glass of milk.

"This is great, really peachy of you to let me in like this. I wish I had some money for you, but I've been thumbing rides for weeks now. All outta dough. Sleeping under the stars."

Phil shoveled in the spaghetti like he hadn't eaten in months. Angeline watched with a mixture of amusement and disgust.

"That's all right. Where are you staying tonight?"

Phil adjusted his collar. "Hadn't thought about it much. I wouldn't mind staying here, if that's okay by you." He raised his eyebrows at her seductively.

"I'm sorry, no. The owners don't allow anyone to stay here without a reservation." Angeline brought his bowl to the sink in the small pantry and wondered if she'd made a mistake by inviting him in.

Angeline whipped around when she felt his footsteps behind her.

"But they wouldn't even have to know." He leaned against the doorway with his hands in his pockets.

"No, that isn't an option. If you're finished, I think it's best that you be on your way," Angeline said. She could feel the hairs on the back her neck begin to rise.

"I do thank you for your hospitality, but I'm not finished quite yet. I think we could have a nice time together if you'd just relax."

"That's it. You need to leave. Now." Anger bubbled beneath the surface. Angeline unconsciously flexed her hand into a fist.

"I'm not goin' anywhere," Phil said, any pretense of being a "nice guy" out the window. He produced a switchblade out of his pocket and extended the blade. "I think it's time you started being a little nicer to me, don't you?"

Angeline couldn't help but smirk. Before he could realize what was happening, Angeline had him pinned against the pantry wall, his head smashed up against a flowery calendar. She sank her teeth into the soft flesh of his neck and smiled as she felt his body go limp. His blood mixed with the sweet tomato sauce from the canned spaghetti was certainly an acquired taste.

When she'd had her fill, she carried him over to the wingback and dropped him into the seat, the upper half of his body draped over the arm. As she watched his fingertips fall still against the pilled carpet, she cocked her head. She really could do this on her own. She'd be just fine with no one to answer to but herself.

CHAPTER TWENTY-TWO

Fog Hollow, Massachusetts, current day

Angeline wondered if she'd said too much. She rubbed her upper arms and grabbed a hoodie from the closet in her entryway. Even though Megan had acted fine after hearing Angeline spill her long and sordid story, that didn't mean she *was* fine. It was a lot for a person to take in. It was a lot for a non-person to take in too. And she hadn't even rehashed all of the gory details.

Everything she'd told her had been the truth. It had been torturous pretending that she didn't feel anything toward Megan, that she didn't see her as anything but a bother that she would move on from once their blood blond had broken. It had gotten weaker over the last month, that much was obvious, but it was still there. Even if it wasn't there anymore, Angeline wasn't sure if she would have told Megan that. If nothing else, it gave Angeline a reason to remain close by.

Megan might have been a nuisance, albeit an incredibly attractive one, in the beginning, but once Angeline had let herself get lost in those gray eyes for more than a second, she knew it would be an uphill battle from there. Megan was sweet and thoughtful and curious, and Angeline hadn't been so attracted someone since...since a very long time ago.

She was afraid, there was no doubt about that. There hadn't

even been a twinge of love for another person in Angeline's heart for decades. She'd honestly believed that that part of her life was over. Done. She'd dedicated herself to the welfare of animals, beings that could actually be trusted, and had decided that she was satisfied with that. One-night stands and the occasional fling had often crossed her path, but nothing more. And that was by design. She supposed she could have tried to find a vampire that she had a spark with, but that felt more like searching for a needle in a haystack than a real possibility. And her last relationship with a vampire had been disastrous.

No, she'd been content. A little empty, maybe, but content. Angeline scrolled through the local news on her phone to see if anything was amiss. Something felt off, though she couldn't put her finger on what, exactly. Her senses weren't exactly piqued, but she was disquieted just the same. It was probably nothing, just the nerves of being with someone like Megan after all the time that had passed. It was momentous, really. But that explanation didn't satisfy her. She opened up the *Sun* to see if anything had been reported, something that would make Nolan seek out Megan again. Local kid wins math bee. Funding for school playground denied. Council on Aging holding meeting on first Thursday of the month.

Murder at Eastbay Park. Angeline sat down at her kitchen table and read the story with a growing pit in her stomach.

Fog Hollow, Massachusetts. UPDATED: 23:41 EST

With no suspects in custody, Fog Hollow is becoming a deadly place to live. Fog Hollow's own journalist Blair Gates came across a disturbing and terrifying image earlier this evening. A local resident, who must remain nameless until the police have finished their investigation, was found beneath one of the wooden benches at Eastbay Park. Gates touched the victim's shoulder to see if they were responsive, only to find that they were not. It appeared to Gates that not only was the victim's left ear missing, but that all blood had been completely drained from the body. There were bite marks and puncture wounds on the victim's face and on their jawline. Fog Hollow police declined to comment. Developing story.

Again. Angeline cringed. That had to be why the detective wanted to see Megan. Anything else would be too coincidental. But really, at this point, how dangerous was too dangerous? Angeline appreciated Megan covering for her, but if the detective was so sure that she knew something, Angeline was afraid that his investigation would intensify. What that meant was a mystery. Angeline had done her very best to evade the law as often as possible over her extensive time on earth. Police would only complicate things. She had to find out who was doing this and, one way or another, put a stop to it. The only person who would have a vendetta against her personally, at least that she knew of, had been dead for a very long time. There was always a niggling part of her that wondered if, somehow, Kathryn had managed to escape the burning house that day, but Angeline didn't see any possible way. She'd been stuck to the heavy door by a sword in the proverbial stone.

Angeline pulled up her messaging app and clicked on Megan. As she began to type, she felt a tug in her chest. Huh. She rubbed aimlessly at the spot, trying to decide if it was an undigested piece of fried chicken or something a little more serious. She picked her phone back up, but before she was able to compose anything coherent, she fell backward into the chair, her stomach cramping in pain. Angeline felt suffocated, terrified, and sweat began to pour down her forehead. She was disoriented for a moment before she realized what the pain signified: Megan.

Angeline felt her fangs jut out in response to the swirling within her body. She willed herself to see past the emotion and get her bearings. Maybe Nolan had arrested her. Angeline refused to allow herself to think anything worse. She had a simple task in front of her. Find Megan and put an end to whatever had frightened her so desperately.

CHAPTER TWENTY-THREE

Megan opened her eyes slowly, blinking rapidly. It took her a minute to recognize her surroundings. She was in her basement, nestled between totes full of Halloween decorations and various vacuums and carpet shampooers that she'd accumulated over the years. She'd meant to either trash them or have them fixed at some point, but she just hadn't gotten around to it.

Before she could wonder what she was doing in her basement on the floor, Megan realized that her hands were tied above her head. Bungee cords, her own from her last trip to Laconia, secured her to the cast iron sewer pipe that snaked its way around the basement. It took a second, but it all came flooding back to her in a nauseating wave. Kathryn, the doorknob, the searing pain in the back of her head. She felt a scream well up, but she successfully pushed it away. She had a feeling it wouldn't do her any good anyway. She looked at the bungee cords again. The top of the cord, near the metal hook, was slightly frayed. Maybe it would provide her with the weakness she needed to break free. She pulled as hard she could, the nylon burning her wrists, but the cord didn't give at all.

"Oh, you're awake. Goody," Kathryn sat flipping through a magazine at Megan's tool bench. It didn't actually contain many tools except for a hammer, a wrench, and a few other assorted items that had come inside the toolkit Aunt Susie had given her a few years ago. Mostly the bench was piled with entertainment magazines meant for recycling and old paint cans.

"What do you want?" Megan asked again, her voice sounding more like a croak than her actual voice.

Kathryn shrugged. "A lot of things. Are you in love with her?"

"Angeline?"

"No, Meryl Streep."

Megan took the hint. "Probably. Why does that matter? Are you going to kill me because you're jealous?"

"Of course not," Kathryn said. "I'm not jealous. And I'm not here to kill *you*. I mean, I probably will, but you're just collateral damage. Sorry about that."

Megan felt the terror begin to creep up her throat again. She didn't know what to do. Should she scream and yell and fight to free herself? Stay quiet and hope that Kathryn would lose interest in whatever little game she was playing and leave them alone? Taunt her? Compliment her? Megan couldn't help but wonder how she had gone thirty plus years without staring death in the face, and now she'd done it twice in just a few months. Something was clearly working against her.

"Why now, though?" Megan asked, deciding keeping Kathryn engaged might be the best course of action.

"She did a very good job of keeping herself hidden over the years. I've come back to Massachusetts a few times looking for her, but she was never where I thought she'd be. That was my mistake, obviously. I should have checked every little hellhole this side of the Rockies. She always was a creature of habit."

Kathryn pulled her hair forward over one shoulder, twisting it in her hands. Megan stared at her, trying to rationalize that the pale, unassuming little redhead was a toxic psychopath with the strength of ten men.

"How did you find her?"

"Fate? Coincidence? Could have been either. I was having a drink in a little pub in Worcester when a news story came on about a robbery in a tiny little town named Fog Hollow. One of the victims was found nearly a mile from the site with no recollection of how she arrived there, and gunshot wounds that weren't visible. And the perpetrator was found with his throat ripped out like an animal had gotten to him. In his truck. With the windows up. I may be a lot of things, but naive isn't one of them. It was quite obviously a vampire. I came to your little town and I sussed her out in no time. I didn't know if I would find Angeline or some infantile baby vamp who didn't know how to cover their tracks. I should have known it would be her, avenging the humans she seems to like so much," Kathryn said, clicking her tongue.

"Why didn't you just go after her when you found her?" Megan asked. She gave another futile tug on the bungee cords just in case they had suddenly loosened up.

"What is this, twenty questions? The first time I saw her, she was with you. Picking you up in some nightclub parking lot. I followed you back here and realized that you two had a thing. I remember that dewy look from our time in New York." Kathryn grimaced. "Charlotte."

Megan briefly closed her eyes. The invocation of that name wasn't exactly comforting.

"Rather than just burn her alive or decapitate her or rip her apart piece by piece, I decided it would be a lot more satisfying to really hurt her. Make her suffer. Have her running scared. You know, all those clichéd things that a bad guy in any horror movie would do. At this point, I couldn't imagine anything better."

"You killed an innocent person to freak her out? Really?"

"People. You're so sentimental. And innocence is subjective. But even if it isn't, what do I care? I didn't know them, and even if I did, I'm sure I wouldn't have liked them." Kathryn shrugged and went back to her magazine. It seemed like question and answer period was officially over.

Megan's muscles were beginning to hurt from being suspended in that upright position without any relief. She searched her immediate vicinity for any sort of weapon, not that it would do any good in her current position. But it would have been nice if she'd had a loaded rifle lying next to her feet. The closest thing she had to anything dangerous was the garden tool organizer hanging on the wall behind Kathryn's head. Megan wasn't sure how a hoe, a rusty pitchfork, a broom, or a dented shovel would hold up against a centuries-old vampire, but her old guillotine paper cutter was on the other side of the tool bench. It had seemed silly to take that—along with about twenty staplers and ten boxes of paper clips—when her old office building had closed, especially since all of those items just sat in the basement untouched. But that could possibly inflict injury if the opportunity arose. The blade looked like a small sword attached to a table, and it was probably still sharp enough to do some damage.

A loud crash made her jump. The door to the basement burst open, planks of wood flying down the stairs like it had exploded. Kathryn was suddenly standing next to Megan, her hand clenched tightly around the back of Megan's neck, even though Megan hadn't even seen her move. She smiled, her fangs glistening in the low light of the basement.

Angeline moved down the stairs at such speed it was as though she was flying. She continued toward Megan and Kathryn and then stopped short, nearly toppling over from the sheer force of her sudden stop.

"No. You're supposed to be dead," Angeline said softly. Her eyes glinted and she covered her teeth with her lips. Megan could see the shock on her face, accented with the slightest bit of panic.

Kathryn chuckled hoarsely. "Clearly, I'm not. Here I am. Live and in person. Have you missed me, Angie? Because I have certainly missed you."

"But I killed you. You burned to death. I saw the flames. I saw the smoke when I drove away."

"Yes, the house was on fire. And holy hell, did that hurt. We may not feel pain in most cases, but when your skin is burning and broiling and liquefying? It fucking hurts." Kathryn eased up on Megan's neck slightly. "Someone was kind enough to call the fire department. A nice man in full gear broke down the door with an axe and was able to pull the sword out of my stomach with some rescue tool he had on him. He brought me outside and laid me on a stretcher. I was a pulpy mess by that point, so I'm lucky he didn't just write me off. By the time he finished searching his first aid kit, I was almost completely healed. I thanked him, of course. And then I had to kill him."

Megan whimpered involuntarily and Angeline flinched.

"What? Can you imagine the questions he would have had? I had no choice. That one is on you too," Kathryn said, pointing to Angeline.

"Why did you wait all this time?" Angeline asked, her hands fisted at her sides.

"I already answered all of this with your chatty girlfriend." Kathryn waved her free hand in condescension. "Your disappearing act worked quite well. I figured with the advent of the internet I'd be able to find you easily. But no, you covered your tracks and did nothing newsworthy, so it was dead end after dead end. I knew you'd end up back here, though. I've been to Lowell more times than I can count over the last six decades. Luckily for you, you weren't *that* stupid."

"You've been looking for me ever since? You've wasted sixty years on a revenge mission?" Angeline asked. She seemed disheartened, almost resigned. Megan watched her carefully.

"Of course. I mean, I've done other things too. You weren't my *sole* focus. But no one, *no one*, can do what you did to me and just walk away."

Megan's eyes met with Angeline's. Angeline took a step toward them and Kathryn tightened her grip exponentially. Megan couldn't help the frightened squeak that made it past Kathryn's clasp.

"Ah-ah," she scolded in a singsong voice. "Like a toothpick, Angeline. Like a toothpick."

Angeline stepped back.

"What do you want?"

"I want you to die. But before that, I want you to feel everything you felt that night all over again. But this time you don't get to walk away."

Angeline blanched but stood firm. "Don't. Please. She did nothing wrong. Your grievance is with me, Kathryn. Let her go, and you and I will finish this."

"No!" Megan whispered.

Kathryn gave her hair a tug, prompting a hiss of pain. Angeline stepped forward again, but heeded Kathryn's warning.

"You know, the more I think about it, I miss having someone around. I've had a few yous over the years, but none of them were able to fill your shoes. Maybe it's time for another Massachusetts girl to fill the void." Kathryn bared her fangs in a maniacal smile and bent toward Megan's neck.

Angeline was on her in a fraction of a second, Kathryn's head clanging against the pipe, though she didn't loosen her hold on Megan even a fraction. She pushed Angeline off her so forcefully that Angeline fell back twenty feet. She scrambled backward until her back hit the bottom stair. She was up again in an instant. "Don't fucking touch her, Kathryn."

"And what, exactly, do you plan to do about it?" Kathryn traced her fingernail along the length of Megan's neck, ending at her chin. "If I want her, I'll have her."

Megan felt tears pool in her eyes. She wondered if she'd ever see Aunt Susie again, and chastised herself for waiting so long in between each visit. And Merlin. Stacey would have to take him. He'd be confused at first, but he'd eventually settle in, and hopefully forget her. It was all too much. This wasn't supposed to happen to a normal person. Megan was supposed to live her life and enjoy a few moments along the way, before it all ended in a very anticlimactic final breath at a ripe old age. Tears began to slide down her cheeks.

"Just get it over with, Kathryn," Angeline said. "Take me.

I won't fight you." She stared at Megan, who couldn't stop the silent sobs that kept coming.

"No, Angeline," Megan said, breathing in deeply. "Don't sacrifice yourself for me. She'll kill me anyway."

Kathryn nodded. "She's got a point. But unless you want me to drive her to the brink over and over again, until she's finally begging me for the sweet release of death, I suggest you come on over here and take a seat." Kathryn pushed one of Megan's old wooden bar stools in front of her.

Megan's chest hitched as she saw Angeline sit on the wobbly stool. Angeline mouthed the words "I'm sorry" and closed her eyes as Kathryn finally let go of Megan and circled Angeline.

"I brought something a little sturdier for you, my dear." Kathryn reached onto the worktop and produced a twenty-foot binder chain with tow hooks on either end. She snapped it tightly for effect.

"You don't need to use that, Kathryn. I already told you I won't fight you."

"Where's the fun in that?"

"So, you're doing this for fun?" Megan asked.

Kathryn didn't respond. Megan tugged futilely one more time. She glanced up toward the ceiling, where the metal clamp holding a few rusty screws jutted out. If she could only extend herself a few inches higher, she might be able to reach it. Even on her tiptoes, she was just shy of the clamp.

Kathryn continued to wrap the chain around Angeline's feet, pontificating about the disadvantages of betraying someone who was kind enough to take a person under their wing. Megan eyed the small suitcase to the left of her that still had the Newark Airport tags on it from a real estate conference she attended a couple of years ago. She kicked her left leg out and was encouraged by the fact that the suitcase rattled a little. She froze, but Kathryn was still focused on Angeline.

"I did what I did to you because of what you did to me. Are

you really so wrapped up in your revenge fantasy that you can't see that? That I hurt you because of how many fucking times you hurt me?" Angeline asked. Kathryn bent so she was eye to eye with Angeline. The chain rested in her hand.

"Do you really think I care? After everything that we'd been through together, you so callously tried to wipe me out of existence over a girl. A *girl*. And not a very worthy one at that."

Megan kicked out again, slightly harder this time. Her toe landed on the hard plastic of the travel bag, and she was able to inch it over to herself, just a hair. It wasn't enough.

"Then just get your revenge, put me out of my misery, and let Megan go. Try to summon that tiniest bit of humanity that you must still have inside you. I saw it back then. Not often, but it was there," Angeline said as Kathryn crisscrossed the chain around her shoulders.

Megan prayed for just another minute or two before Kathryn turned to her with the intent to kill. She wasn't asking to be rescued, just asking for one more minute. She let out a loud sob as she dragged the suitcase over just a little bit more. It was enough. Maybe.

Kathryn turned to her, so Megan dropped her head in sorrow, letting her hands drape loosely over one another. Would Kathryn notice that the suitcase had moved by a few inches? Megan wept loudly again, hoping for any distraction that would keep Kathryn focused on her body and not the space around her.

"Any humanity I had left drifted away with the smoke that night in New York, Angeline. You showed me what I had always known. Trust and loyalty are figments of the imagination. A nice notion, but not real. You need to keep quiet," Kathryn said, still staring at Megan. "I'm sure you'll feel bad if I need to tear out a neighbor's throat for poking around to see what all this commotion is about."

"Sorry," Megan choked out, relieved that Kathryn turned back to Angeline. She felt a rush of adrenaline course through her and, for the first time since listening to Aunt Susie's message on the answering machine, had the slightest inkling that she and Angeline might live to spend another night together.

Kathryn walked over to where she had kept the chain and picked up a closed shackle padlock. "If you can break through this, then I'll serve myself to you on a platter," Kathryn said. She chuckled and fiddled with the key, trying to open the heavy lock.

Megan's stomach flipped as she pressed her toes onto the very edge of the suitcase. It gave her just the height advantage she needed, and she tried to silently raise her arms toward the protruding screw. Angeline caught her eyes and widened her own. Her hands were shaking profusely, which didn't help her aim. She'd moved the frayed part of the bungee just below the screw when she felt a crushing blow to her stomach. Megan exhaled, groaning in pain, her body nearly bent in half, held up only by her bound arms. The world in front of her grayed out for just a moment before coming back into a blurry kind of focus.

"Are you *that* fucking stupid? Really?" Kathryn asked, running her tongue along the tips of her fangs. She grabbed Megan by the back of the neck and sank her teeth into the soft flesh above her collarbone.

Megan screamed in shock and agony as her flesh was breached by the tiny daggers. She gripped Kathryn's shoulders, trying to push her away, but she didn't budge. Megan felt her arms grow limp around Kathryn's neck.

Until Kathryn was suddenly ripped off her, her teeth dragging painful tracks up the length of Megan's neck. Kathryn screamed gutturally as she was slammed up against the hard metal of the oil tank. Angeline wrapped a length of chain around her neck and pulled tightly while Kathryn clawed at her.

"You should have locked it first, asshole," Angeline growled. She continued to pull on the chain around Kathryn's neck.

Megan tried to catch the suitcase with her toe again, but Kathryn had pushed it too far out of the way. Blinding pain continued to explode from the wound on her neck, but she knew she had to push past it if they had any hope of getting out of this alive.

Angeline looked over at her. Megan shook her head, trying to give Angeline a silent sign to keep doing what she was doing. *Don't worry about me. I'm not going anywhere, obviously.*

It was the distraction Kathryn needed. In a burst of energy, she brought up her knee and slammed it directly into Angeline's midsection.

"No!" Megan cried as Angeline stumbled backward. Before Kathryn could latch on to her, Angeline reached up and pulled on the bungee cords securing Megan to the pipe. She used so much force that the pipe dislodged from the wall and the cord snapped in two. Megan fell to her knees as Kathryn lifted Angeline off the ground like she was a toddler.

When Kathryn slammed Angeline to the concrete floor, Megan was sure she heard the bones in Angeline's back fracture. Megan lurched over to where Kathryn had Angeline pinned. She grabbed the steel shovel from the wall and slammed it into the back of Kathryn's head.

Kathryn shrieked in pain but didn't move off Angeline. She sank her teeth into Angeline's neck, tearing the flesh as she shook her head back and forth like a wild animal.

"Megan, run!" Angeline yelled, her tone urgent and garbled.

"What the hell is going on here?" a deep, booming voice called from the top of the stairs.

Megan's head, as well as Kathryn's, whipped around to see who was coming down the stairs. Detective Nolan walked slowly toward them with his gun drawn.

"Get up and I want to see your hands in the air," Nolan said, training his gun on Kathryn.

Kathryn's face broke out into a grim smile. "You ever heard of wrong place, wrong time?"

Kathryn looked at Angeline, who lay beneath her, motionless

and bleeding, her eyes closed. She moved off her and made her way toward Nolan.

"Stop or I will shoot you!" he yelled.

She continued walking slowly toward him, her eyes glinting like the predator she was, blood dripping from her chin. Nolan cocked his gun.

"What the fuck?" he said as Kathryn opened her mouth to reveal her fangs. Megan covered her ears as Nolan discharged his weapon, four bullets in all. Kathryn didn't stop walking toward him, though she winced in pain as each bullet breached her skin.

Megan raised the shovel to hit Kathryn again, mustering all of her strength. Before she could bring the cutting edge down on her head, she felt Angeline rush by her with ethereal speed. She impaled Kathryn from behind with Megan's pitchfork, producing a gurgled scream of outrage from Kathryn. Kathryn looked down in horror at the sharp points of the pitchfork protruding through her chest. Nolan scrambled backward up the stairs so fast, he tore the leg of his dress pants. Megan rushed over to the tool bench and detached the sharp blade from the paper cutter.

"This is it, Kathryn. Finished," Angeline said, her neck still bleeding from the gushing wound Kathryn had created. "I won't leave any *maybes* this time around."

Kathryn gripped one of the tines of the pitchfork, the one protruding through the area of her heart. She couldn't reach the handle to pull the tines from her chest. "You have a fondness for impalement, don't you? Just leave me this way, Angeline. You know I can't harm you like this. Take your girl and go far away. I'll let you live. Both of you."

Angeline stood behind Kathryn, still holding tightly to the pitchfork. "You're a liar, Kathryn."

"No, I'm not. Not this time. You've proven yourself. I can't beat you."

"You're right, you can't," Megan said, her hands shaking. She handed the shredder blade to Angeline. Megan had watched enough true crime shows and read enough books to know that decapitating someone wasn't as easy as it looked on TV. Angeline had to be the one to do it.

Angeline looked at Megan, her eyes shining. Megan nodded sadly. She didn't want to see anyone beheaded, but how could they be sure Kathryn wouldn't go back on her word? Based on the very limited knowledge that Megan had of her, Kathryn allowing them to go on peacefully was highly unlikely.

"Why won't she die?" Nolan asked, his gun pointed directly at Kathryn's head. He didn't seem to understand that was an exercise in futility, as the preceding bullets had done virtually no damage. And he looked more than a little rattled, his eyes wide and his grip on the gun making his knuckles white.

"Because I'm a vampire, you dumb shit. Angeline, pull this out of me, it hurts. Come on," Kathryn said. She sucked in a breath between her teeth.

"I can't let you go, Kathryn. You have to know that," Angeline said. Tears tracked down her cheeks, but she never looked away.

Kathryn nodded, her head tilted as she looked at Angeline like she was seeing her for the first time. "I get it. Do what you have to do." Kathryn leaned forward, holding on to the tines and seeming to brace herself for the inevitable.

Angeline hesitated.

"Do it," Nolan whispered.

Megan closed her eyes but opened them again when she heard a shout.

Kathryn threw herself forward and down, the motion jerking the handle out of Angeline's hands. She landed face down on the cement, the pitchfork releasing itself from her body by the hard push of the tines against the ground. She was up in a flash and screeching toward Angeline. But Angeline was ready.

Megan ducked even though the swish sound of the blade cutting through the air was nowhere near her. Angeline arced the paper cutter blade with her right hand and caught Kathryn right beneath the ear. Megan expected to hear screams and slicing and the squirting of blood, but she heard nothing except for a muted thud.

Kathryn's body fell to its knees before collapsing completely forward. Her head lay next to her hand, where the ring finger continued to twitch for a full second before falling still.

Megan covered her mouth, unable to look away from the carnage in front of her. On her basement floor. It didn't look real. The head looked more like a grotesque doll's head, with its staring eyes and red lips, than a dead vampire who had been actively trying to kill them all.

Angeline rushed over to Megan and drew her close. Megan buried her head in Angeline's shoulder and wept.

"Are you okay?" Angeline whispered, softly caressing Megan's hair. She touched her fingertips to the drying blood on Megan's neck.

Megan nodded, sniffling. She flinched at the light pressure on her neck. "Are you?"

"Mostly." Angeline craned her neck so Megan could see the damage. It was still raw and bleeding from Kathryn's teeth. "But don't worry about me." She inspected Megan's neck again. "It doesn't look like she did any lethal damage, thankfully. You'll probably have a scar, though, unless I try to heal you right now. I'm a little weak at the moment, but I should be able to muster enough strength to take care of you."

"Really, I'm okay. It hurts, but a scar is the least of my worries right now. Why aren't you healing?"

"A wound from a vampire bite is a lot harder to heal from. It will take time." Angeline squeezed her tightly.

Megan squeezed back, trying to decide if what she'd just witnessed was real or if she'd truly lost her mind. The pain in her neck was very real, as were Angeline's arms around her.

"Ahem." Nolan cleared his throat, in a not-so-subtle attempt to divert Angeline's and Megan's attention from each other.

"Oh, Detective Nolan. Told you I wasn't making it up."

Megan shrugged, and if there weren't a dead, beheaded vampire on the floor in front of her, she would have laughed at Nolan's bewildered expression.

"So, you're Angeline? Megan's vampire savior from the night at the gas station?" Nolan asked, finally standing up from his safe haven on the basement stairs. He straightened his tie.

"I am, yes. And I want you to know, I had nothing to do with that gas station employee or the body you found last night. That was Kathryn," Angeline said, shooting a look at Kathryn's headless body.

"Another body?" Megan asked, looking from Angeline to Nolan and back again.

Nolan nodded. Repeatedly. "Right." He nodded to Kathryn's body and wiped at his forehead. "For now, I'd like to keep this whole thing under wraps. I'm, uh, a little unsure of things at the moment. I need to go home and have a few beers. Hug my wife. Then I'd like to speak to you. Both of you."

"I'm not so sure that's a good idea, Detective—"

He held up a hand. "Megan, it's fine. You're not in any trouble. At least I don't think you are. But I need to know what happened here tonight and what this means. Even if I have to die with the secret, I have to know."

Megan started to protest again, but Angeline put a hand on her shoulder. "That's not a problem, Detective. We'll cooperate with you. But I need a guarantee that you won't send a torch-carrying mob with stakes and crosses to come find me."

"You have my word." Nolan shook his head. "I think I'll keep this to myself. Can you come to the station in the morning?"

"Um, no, the morning doesn't really work for me."

"Right, right. The whole…" Nolan trailed off, waving his arm in a vague motion around the room. "Tomorrow evening, then."

"Sure."

"What's going to happen to this?" Nolan asked, motioning toward Kathryn's body.

"It'll be disposed of properly, I assure you."

"Uh-huh. Okay. Don't tell me anything else, please." Nolan walked back up the stairs, straightening his already straightened tie. He mumbled something incoherent and then Megan heard her front door shut.

"What do we do?" Megan asked, rubbing her forehead. A dead body in her basement was certainly a first.

"I'll take care of it. Go upstairs and make sure Merlin is okay." Angeline grabbed a half-folded tarp from one of Megan's shelves. She picked up the shovel from the floor. "I don't think a bonfire out back would be the best idea. But I'll be in the backyard if you need me. Two separate plots, just in case. Go ahead, really."

Megan bit her lip but turned toward the staircase. She was still in a fog, but it was thankfully beginning to lift. The fallout from what she'd witnessed would probably linger for a while, but she had to remember that there was no other option. Kathryn was a bad vampire; Angeline was a good one. It was that simple, and that weird. She touched her neck again and felt the mark that would become a permanent reminder of a world she didn't even know existed such a short time ago. Nothing would ever be the same again. The thought brought a fleeting feeling of loss, but also one of hope. She felt bad for leaving Angeline alone, but she also didn't really want to be a part of digging a grave in her own backyard. After everything that had happened, Megan knew one thing for certain—the house was going on the market Monday morning.

CHAPTER TWENTY-FOUR

"You're really, really sure? That it was outside the property line?" Megan asked, stretching the packing tape over the last box in the living room.

Angeline nodded. "For the fiftieth time, yes. I made sure it was out in the wetlands behind the house. I've even looked at the survey and used a measuring tape to confirm it."

"I know, I know. I just don't want to be contacted by the buyers a year from now when they try to do some gardening. The lawsuit would be *epic*."

Merlin meowed at his food dish, which was on top of the counter in a bag with his food and treats. He was formally moving into the log cabin before Megan, which wasn't going to happen until the official closing took place the following day. It had only taken two weeks for her house to sell, but by the time the mortgage and everything else was settled with the new buyers, nearly three months had lapsed since that night in the basement. Not that she'd spent more than another night or two in it from that moment forward. She couldn't be there without remembering every moment of the harrowing night. But at Angeline's she was safe and loved, and that was all she needed. Still, she couldn't help still checking her wrists for phantom rope burn every now and then.

"Sit with me for a minute," Angeline said, motioning for

Megan to join her on a blanket on the floor. All of the furniture she was taking had been moved to Angeline's already. Everything else would go after the signing.

"I still can't believe this is it. I thought I'd be here until I was old and gray," Megan said, stretching out next to Angeline. She rested her head on Angeline's shoulder and drew lazy circles on her palm.

Angeline stroked Megan's hair. "I told you that you didn't have to sell. I could have moved the body."

"No! The memories are still there. The visuals. I'd never be fully comfortable here ever again. Besides, I couldn't be any more excited about this next chapter of my life," Megan said. She leaned up and kissed Angeline.

"Me too. And you're still sure that you don't feel like we're moving too fast? Three months isn't a lot of time before moving in together. I don't want you to feel pressured in any way."

"Oh stop. Stacey and Kristen moved in together within a few weeks. It happens. It might not work for everyone, but I'm pretty sure we'll be fine. We've been spending every waking second together anyway, so what's the difference?" Megan smiled as Merlin snuggled up next to them on the blanket.

"You're right. Kristen keeps texting me links to Pinterest for housewarming gift ideas. I told her over and over that they don't need to buy us anything. It's not like we don't have double of *everything*. I mean, how many toasters can two people have?"

"Aw, they're just trying to be a part of it. Stacey asked me if we'd like a bat house for one of the trees out front. I told her it was a little too on the nose, but I think having bats fly overhead every night might actually be sort of cool," Megan said with a shrug.

"I'm not opposed to it. I'd be like their queen. Only in my mind, but still."

Angeline's phone danced across the floor as it vibrated. She reached over and silenced it, tucking it into her back pocket.

"That was just Nolan. He's got some case in the city he wants me to consult on. He thinks I can identify tracks or something like that," Angeline said. She chuckled softly. "I swear, he thinks I'm a German shepherd."

"You *did* help him with that kidnapping last month. Or kidnapping hoax, I should say. I think you should get a badge," Megan said. She squeezed Angeline's thigh.

"I highly doubt that's going to happen anytime soon. Imagine trying to explain a hire like me to the chief. Only available at night. Can't get too worked up. Special diet."

Megan laughed. "I still think you should be recognized for your outstanding service to the state. And I think it's sexy that you're a police consultant on paranormal cases." She pulled Angeline's face down to hers, kissing her deeply. Merlin sensed the movement and jumped onto one of the boxes.

Angeline pushed Megan gently onto the floor and shifted so she was nearly on top of her. They explored each other for the last time under the roof on Shaw Way.

"Mmm," Megan murmured, her heart beating high and hard and fast. "You do know you'll eventually have to turn me, right?"

Angeline raised her head. "Is this really the time to talk about that?"

Megan ran her hand down Angeline's back, her fingertips playing at the waistline on Angeline's jeans. "I can't think of any better time, can you?"

"Only about a million," Angeline said, taking her bottom lip between her teeth. "What happens if you decide you don't really like me all that much ten, thirty, fifty years from now? Oh…that feels good. You'll be stuck drinking blood and living for all eternity, yearning for a normal existence. And you'll resent me." Angeline kissed her again, their lips like magnets.

Megan smiled into the kiss. "Or we could be the greatest love story ever told. Together for infinity, adapting into new people who fall in love again every millennium." Megan sucked in a breath as Angeline's hand found its way underneath her shirt.

"Well, when you say it like that, you make it hard to say no.

But let's revisit this in a decade or so, okay? I don't need to turn you into the undead to prove my love for you. I can do that right here, right now."

Megan grinned, but redirected Angeline's wandering hands. "What if I get hit by a bus before that? Then you'd have to live with that for eternity, and I'd be...dead."

"I'd save you."

"What if you weren't with me when it happened?"

"I'll renew our blood bond, sound good?" Angeline asked. She was clearly losing her limited amount of self-control.

"That would work if you were close by, but what if I was in New York at some financial conference and you were stuck here dealing with a distemper outbreak? You'd never get to me in time. So again, dead." Megan tugged lightly on Angeline's hair, her own restraint waning fast as Angeline's lips trailed down her neck.

Angeline grabbed on to the back of Megan's neck. Her fangs jutted out and her eyes were alight. Megan gasped in response.

"You're right," Angeline said, her voice low. "I'll turn you right now, so we don't have to worry about your impending death ever again." She leaned forward and nipped lightly at the skin covering Megan's jugular.

"Wait!" Megan yelled. "No, don't! Not yet!"

Angeline pulled back, her teeth back to normal but her eyes still shining. She laughed. "That's what I thought. Can we continue, or would you like to keep discussing?" She lay flat on her back and beckoned Megan to her.

Megan sighed in relief and fell into Angeline's waiting arms. Maybe she wasn't ready for that just yet. "I love you."

Megan dissolved in Angeline's strong embrace. Her heartbeat quickened as Angeline stared at her with adoration in her eyes.

"I love you too," she said. She looked at Megan thoughtfully. "And I think you saved me."

"From what?" Megan asked, running her thumb along the line of Angeline's eyebrow.

"From this silent chaos I didn't even know I was existing in. Your love has made me see the world a little bit differently. Maybe everything *doesn't* have to end horribly, I don't know. You, Megan," Angeline said, kissing her gently on the nose, "are the hero of my story."

Megan melted and kissed Angeline softly on the lips. "And to think, this is just the beginning. Not to be presumptuous or anything, but being with you gives a whole new meaning to the idea of forever."

"That's true," Angeline said, smiling. "People say that kind of thing all the time. But with me, you know it's not just an empty word. Only a vampire can *actually* love you forever."

About the Author

Nicole Stiling lives in New England with her wife, two children, and a menagerie of dogs, cats, and fish. When she's not working at her day job or pounding away at the keyboard, she enjoys video games, comic books, clearing out the DVR, and the occasional amusement park. Nicole is a strict vegetarian who does not like vegetables, and a staunch advocate for anything with four legs.

Books Available From Bold Strokes Books

Brooklyn Summer by Maggie Cummings. When opposites attract, can a summer of passion and adventure lead to a lifetime of love? (978-1-63555-578-3)

City Kitty and Country Mouse by Alyssa Linn Palmer. Pulled in two different directions, can a city kitty and a country mouse fall in love and make it work? (978-1-63555-553-0)

Elimination by Jackie D. When a dangerous homegrown terrorist seeks refuge with the Russian mafia, the team will be put to the ultimate test. (978-1-63555-570-7)

In the Shadow of Darkness by Nicole Stiling. Angeline Vallencourt is a reluctant vampire who must decide what she wants more—obscurity, revenge, or the woman who makes her feel alive. (978-1-63555-624-7)

On Second Thought by C. Spencer. Madisen is falling hard for Rae. Even single life and co-parenting are beginning to click. At least, that is, until her ex-wife begins to have second thoughts. (978-1-63555-415-1)

Out of Practice by Carsen Taite. When attorney Abby Keane discovers the wedding blogger tormenting her client is the woman she had a passionate, anonymous vacation fling with, sparks and subpoenas fly. Legal Affairs: one law firm, three best friends, three chances to fall in love. (978-1-63555-359-8)

Providence by Leigh Hays. With every click of the shutter, photographer Rebekiah Kearns finds it harder and harder to keep Lindsey Blackwell in focus without getting too close. (978-1-63555-620-9)

Taking a Shot at Love by KC Richardson. When academic and athletic worlds collide, will English professor Celeste Bouchard and basketball coach Lisa Tobias ignore their attraction to achieve their professional goals? (978-1-63555-549-3)

Flight to the Horizon by Julie Tizard. Airline captain Kerri Sullivan and flight attendant Janine Case struggle to survive an emergency water landing and overcome dark secrets to give love a chance to fly. (978-1-63555-331-4)

In Helen's Hands by Nanisi Barrett D'Arnuk. As her mistress, Helen pushes Mickey to her sensual limits, delivering the pleasure only a BDSM lifestyle can provide her. (978-1-63555-639-1)

Jamis Bachman, Ghost Hunter by Jen Jensen. In Sage Creek, Utah, a poltergeist stirs to life and past secrets emerge.(978-1-63555-605-6)

Moon Shadow by Suzie Clarke. Add betrayal, season with survival, then serve revenge smokin' hot with a sharp knife. (978-1-63555-584-4)

Spellbound by Jean Copeland and Jackie D. When the supernatural worlds of good and evil face off, love might be what saves them all. (978-1-63555-564-6)

Temptation by Kris Bryant. Can experienced nanny Cassie Miller deny her growing attraction and keep her relationship with her boss professional? Or will they sidestep propriety and give in to temptation? (978-1-63555-508-0)

The Inheritance by Ali Vali. Family ties bring Tucker Delacroix and Willow Vernon together, but they could also tear them, and any chance they have at love, apart. (978-1-63555-303-1)

Thief of the Heart by MJ Williamz. Kit Hanson makes a living seducing rich women in casinos and relieving them of the expensive jewelry most won't even miss. But her streak ends when she meets beautiful FBI agent Savannah Brown. (978-1-63555-572-1)

Face Off by PJ Trebelhorn. Hockey player Savannah Wells rarely spends more than a night with any one woman, but when photographer Madison Scott buys the house next door, she's forced to rethink what she expects out of life. (978-1-63555-480-9)

Hot Ice by Aurora Rey, Elle Spencer, and Erin Zak. Can falling in love melt the hearts of the iciest ice queens? Join Aurora Rey, Elle Spencer, and Erin Zak to find out! A contemporary romance novella collection. (978-1-63555-513-4)

Line of Duty by VK Powell. Dr. Dylan Carlyle's professional and personal life is turned upside down when a tragic event at Fairview Station pits her against ambitious, handsome police officer Finley Masters. ((978-1-63555-486-1)

London Undone by Nan Higgins. London Craft reinvents her life after reading a childhood letter to her future self and, in doing so, finds the love she truly wants. (978-1-63555-562-2)

Lunar Eclipse by Gun Brooke. Moon De Cruz lives alone on an uninhabited planet after being shipwrecked in space. Her life changes forever when Captain Beaux Lestarion's arrival threatens the planet and Moon's freedom. (978-1-63555-460-1)

One Small Step by MA Binfield. In this contemporary romance, Iris and Cam discover the meaning of taking chances and following your heart, even if it means getting hurt. (978-1-63555-596-7)

Shadows of a Dream by Nicole Disney. Rainn has the talent to take her rock band all the way, but falling in love is a powerful distraction, and her new girlfriend's meth addiction might just take them both down. 978-1-63555-598-1)

Someone to Love by Jenny Frame. When Davina Trent is given an unexpected family, can she let nanny Wendy Darling teach her to open her heart to the children and to Wendy? (978-1-63555-468-7)

Uncharted by Robyn Nyx. As Rayne Marcellus and Chase Stinsen track the legendary Golden Trinity, they must learn to put their differences aside and depend on one another to survive. (978-1-63555-325-3)

Where We Are by Annie McDonald. A sensual account of two women who discover a way to walk on the same path together with the help of an Indigenous tale, a Canadian art movement, and the mysterious appearance of dimes. (978-1-63555-581-3)